WHERE THE NIGHT REIGNS

In the Darkness, Book Three

Emilie Lucadamo

A NineStar Press Publication

Published by NineStar Press
P.O. Box 91792,
Albuquerque, New Mexico, 87199 USA.
www.ninestarpress.com

Where the Night Reigns

Copyright © 2019 by Emilie Lucadamo
Cover Art by Natasha Snow Copyright © 2019

Printed in the USA
First Edition
July, 2019

Print ISBN: 978-1-951057-06-0

Also available in eBook, ISBN: 978-1-951057-05-3

Warning: This book contains depictions of demonic possession, battle scenes, and character death.

The barrier between worlds has shattered. Demons wreak havoc across Earth; the dead are rising from their graves; psychics and witches are vanishing without a trace. The fate of the world rests in the hands of the enigmatic Tresser Corporation, a company of demon soldiers... and a kindergarten teacher.

In other words, humanity's odds aren't looking great.

When hunter, David Tresser, pairs up with a High Demon, he knows he's in over his head. Of course, there are worse positions to be in, like Henry, whose girlfriend hasn't been seen since the demonic attacks began, or the psychic Cassandra, who has become a target of those very demons herself. As this motley crew teams up, trust is slow to be gained...but they really have no choice when the world around them is falling apart at the seams. In the midst of it all, Tresser finds himself curiously drawn to the demon he's not even sure he can trust.

After an exorcism gone terribly wrong, the team is left with no choice. To save their worlds, and themselves, they'll have to travel into the darkest part of Hell: the Pits of Gehenna, from which no one has ever returned.

To defeat the odds and preserve humanity, they'll all have to work together.

For Madison, the fireworks, and a thousand
glittering dawns rising over the Sound.

Chapter One

THE TEA HAS long since gone cold, but Tresser swirls it around his cup anyway. He's not about to take a sip. It is far too frigid, and the last thing he wants to do is wind up spewing liquid over all this cozy living room upholstery.

At least that might give his host a valid excuse to kick him out. Then again, Cassandra Carlyle might be too damn nice—or too appeased by the Tresser Corporation's considerable paycheck—to do it.

It's obvious Cassandra isn't happy having him here. That could have something to do with the fact that Tresser pulled up unannounced in front of her pleasant country home in a hearse.

(The ride is none-too-inconspicuous. His father had been adamant against it. Naturally, that's why Tresser had to have it. It's proved itself useful in carting around things such as equipment or bodies and has the *most comfortable* reclining seats.)

To be fair to her, Cassandra has taken it in stride. She let Tresser in, made him tea, and when he said they needed to talk, her reply was a gamely, "I've got the time."

It's still obvious she doesn't want him here. Her wary gaze keeps flickering to Tresser's dark boots like she expects them to leave oily imprints on the carpet. Her posture is a bit too relaxed, and her smile a bit too pleasant for her to be genuinely pleased with the company. Despite this, Tresser is impressed. Cassandra is good at concealing her displeasure under a veneer of easygoing friendliness. If figuring out what people are hiding weren't his job, Tresser would never have known the difference.

"I'm not sure what to say, Mr. Tresser," Cassandra sighs. Her fingers are wrapped around her teacup, violet painted nails stark against the white porcelain. "It's all a lot to handle."

If anyone can handle the chaos their world is descending into, Tresser is sure it will be Cassandra. The woman has already figured out how to deal with him. If she's that good, she could probably walk through fire and brimstone without flinching.

"I've had to perform more exorcisms in the past few weeks than in ten *years*. News outlets are losing their heads. Buildings are being destroyed, people are dying, and our city is at the epicenter of it all." She swallows, gaze flickering down for a second, and Tresser knows she wants to say something critical. She swallows it back at the last moment, however, settling for a mild but pointed, "It's a good thing Tresser Corporation is here to take care of it."

Except Tresser Corporation *isn't*, not really. If the Corps were really focused on this tiny Rhode Island city, barely a speck on the map, then the problem would be over with by now. Men in black suits and sunglasses would swarm the streets; news outlets would be silent on the chaos, and common mediums wouldn't be the ones performing exorcisms.

Tresser Corporation is currently focused on some tiny European country, which is being controlled by a dictator possessed by a demon of *Ars Goetia* lore. This wouldn't be a major cause for concern, except the dictator has nukes, and that's the sort of apocalypse even the Corps aren't equipped to deal with. As long as the war in Hell stays mostly confined to Hell, Felix Tresser declared, it wasn't any of their business. So instead of centering his focus on the tiny city literally crumbling to hell, he jetted off to Europe and sent a handful of his agents down to deal with it.

The crisis proved to be more than the agents were equipped to deal with, however. Only a week later, chaotic mission reports were being sent back to Felix—details of demonic possessions and people coming back from the dead. It became clear this was far more serious than it appeared on the surface.

That was when Tresser received the command to get down to Rhode Island and see what was what. This order came in the form of an e-mail—since his father was clearly too busy to call—with the mission reports attached.

Tresser wishes he could say he's surprised, but after twenty-six years he knows the way his father's world works.

More surprising, he supposes, is the fact that his father trusted him enough to place him in charge of this operation at all. Had this come at any other time, Felix would have handled something of this magnitude himself. Instead, he's been forced to appoint his son, and Tresser would be lying if he said he was prepared. He's led missions before, but nothing like this.

A part of him had no clue where to start, so as soon as he got into town he went for the obvious—a list of Tresser Corps' contacts throughout the city. He found two names, and Cassandra Carlyle was the first on his list.

"I need you," he said as soon as he sat down with the psychic, "to explain exactly what the hell's been going on here."

Now, with Cassandra wrapping up her sordid tale—full of destruction, chaos, and more demons than an exorcist could shake a cross at—Tresser wonders again whether he's in over his head.

He's as good at hiding his discontent as Cassandra is, if not better (years of dealing with his father has given him time to practice). Sure, in his rumpled jeans and leather jacket Tresser might not look the part of a typical Corps agent, he's got his own brain behind him—plus, an abundance of resources to work with. A lot can be said about David Tresser, but only one person has ever dared call him incompetent, and that man just put him in charge of saving this entire city.

And, if what Cassandra is telling him is true, maybe the world. But Felix doesn't need to know that until later.

As Cassandra finally falls silent, the expression on her face is clear: expectant. Tresser has said he's here to help, and Cassandra is trusting him to do just that.

He knows exactly where to start.

"Okay," Tresser says, clapping his hands together in a faux-eager gesture that makes Cassandra grimace. "I guess this makes you my eyes and ears."

Cassandra blinks. Of all the things she may have expected, that wasn't one of them. "I'm...sorry? What are you talking about?"

"You. You're a psychic, and a medium. That makes you doubly qualified to give me the information I need to know." Tresser Corps employs psychics for just this purpose; during a mission, they can be crucial for obtaining information that would otherwise have remained unknown. If Cassandra weren't skilled, the Corps would never have bothered with her. "You're going to help me out."

"Mr. Tresser—" Cassandra begins, but Tresser cuts her off as he stands up.

"*That's* my father. If you have to be formal, Tresser works just fine. Drop the 'mister', I'm not your boss."

Cassandra follows him as he makes his way to the door. "I think I'm just confused about what you're asking."

"Scrying, right?" Tresser demands lightly. "You can scry."

"Of course I can, but—"

"Great!" Tresser claps the woman on the shoulder—and, realizing at the last moment that he's still holding the teacup, presses it back into her hands. "I'll call you later. Sometime. Wait for me. Tresser Corporations thanks you for your assistance!"

The last comment is smarmy enough to make his father proud. Tresser has read the script enough times to know what to say when making an associate do something they might not want to do. He isn't taking advantage of Cassandra; he just needs a psychic's insight, and she's been helpful so far.

She's getting paid. She'll get over it.

Tresser strides out the front door before Cassandra can get another word in. He's not halfway down the walkway before the door slams shut behind him, loud enough to make the windows shake. Tresser springs a foot into the air, landing hard and casting an incredulous look back at the house. No way was that *his* fault, and he's sure Cassandra didn't do it.

He shakes his head as he double-times it towards his hearse. Damn mediums—always living in haunted houses.

HE'S NOT IN the supermarket for food.

It's not like he needs to buy a rotisserie chicken or mashed potatoes. The hearse is well-stocked with everything he needs to hold him out for a week, at least— canned food, boxes of saltines, bags of junk snacks, and enough booze to kill a horse. There's also a healthy amount of takeout places in town, and if he tips enough, he knows the delivery guys bring it straight to his car.

Tresser eyes a box of Instant Whatever before tossing it into his shopping cart. He isn't interested in groceries.

He narrows his eyes at the end of the aisle where a few cashiers are clustered together. It's obvious that they're not working; at least, they aren't doing whatever their jobs ought to be. No doubt they're working something else, but Tresser doesn't feel like letting them get that far. When you have a problem with weeds, you cut them off at their root. Tresser isn't a gardener.

He weighs a box of cheese crackers in his hand before starting down the aisle. "Excuse me! Can I get some help?"

One of the cashiers looks up. Tresser chucks the box right at his head.

It's a direct hit. The blow glances off the center of the man's skull, and his eyes flare black for a split second before he tumbles over. There's no time to feel victorious. The other three demons are on him in the next second, bounding across the aisle with superhuman speed. Tresser is ready for them.

One is sent flying over his shoulder. The next gets an arm around him, but Tresser does a quick twist and hurls him into the nearest shelf. The third one reaches him as he's throwing them off and wraps both arms around his neck.

There is the momentary flash of panic that comes with his airway being cut off. Tresser drowns that out; he reaches for the bag of salt open in the seat of his shopping cart, catches up a handful, and flings it over his shoulder.

The demon tumbles back with an unholy hiss. Tresser gasps in a deep breath, and knees him in the groin.

With all three demons immobile at his feet, he makes quick work of them. He pulls a marker out of his pocket, a vial of holy water from his shirt, and gets to work.

"Vasa sacra purifica," he recites, eyes narrowing in annoyance rather than focus. *"Retro ad te ipsum."*

Once the demons are gone, he doesn't wait around for the clerks to wake up. After one more quick exorcism at the end of the aisle, he's good to go.

He's two seconds from leaving when he stops, approaches the nearest (human) clerk, and holds up the box of cheese crackers from before. "Hey, can I buy these in bulk?"

Other than that, Tresser's afternoon goes pretty smoothly.

HE WISHES HE could say he knows the car is occupied by demons thanks to some supernatural gift—a psychic sense granting him the ability to detect demons with only a glance. Or he could just be *that good*—able to tell by the way a demon walks, or talks, or even smells. (Agent Markowicz from Exorcism Affairs is revered for his ability to "feel" demons, but almost everyone in the Corps agrees that, psychic or not, he's nuts.)

It isn't anything like that. Tresser knows demons are driving the car the moment it nearly plows straight into a tree.

Demons can't drive. It's a known fact among anyone worth their salt as an exorcist or demonologist. They just don't know *how*. In Hell, there are no roads, and cars are an invention of the far-off human world that they have little interest in. Whenever demons cross the barrier and wind up behind the wheel of a car, they always prove themselves foreigners in the worst ways.

(It's hilarious. Tresser remembers the one time a demon he was chasing drove into the ocean, convinced the car's wheels would keep him afloat. He was wrong.)

He wishes all it took to cure every terrible driver was an exorcism, but life isn't that simple. Still, one glance makes it clear that this driver—Tresser catches a flash of a determined-looking man behind the wheel—has no clue what he's doing. The car careens down the otherwise-deserted road like its engine is on fire, spinning off into a bush and narrowly avoiding a tree, only to drive on unfazed. Tresser has seen bad drivers (hell, he's been his *sister's* passenger) but only a demon drives like that.

It's late enough at night that the hearse blends into the shadows. Tresser revs the engine and starts off down the road. He keeps his lights off, following the brightly lit specter of the Jeep up ahead. He's been drinking since early this afternoon, and by this point he wouldn't call himself sober, but his driving is nowhere near as erratic as the car in front of him. With one hand he steers the car, while the other dials a familiar number.

"Hope it's not past your bedtime," he greets as soon as the line picks up. "I need to take advantage of your considerable talent."

"I was about to have dinner," Cassandra replies over the line, sounding disappointed.

"Hmm, something good?"

"Soup."

"It can wait. Get your crystal ball out, I need you to scry on someone for me."

He hears a huff over the other end of the line, the psychic muttering under her breath as she presumably digs out the tools of her trade. Only when Tresser hears a noisy clang, like a metal pot hitting the ground, does he deign to ask, "Do you actually have a crystal ball?"

"It's easier than water scrying," Cassandra replies. "Hang on, just let me light these candles."

The car in front of Tresser swerves alarmingly, coming close to reeling off the road. Recovering, it switches into reverse and doubles back at least ten feet. Keeping a safe distance away, Tresser makes a face and hopes neither person in the car is prone to carsickness. Just watching makes him queasy.

"Could you hurry up a bit with that? I'm one sharp turn from going off-road here."

"You ask for my help, you learn to be patient," Cassandra shoots back, an edge of annoyance finally creeping into her voice. Tresser grins. After a few more seconds (the car has started up the road, with Tresser following) Cassandra gives an affirmative hum. "Okay, ready."

"Okay. The plate number is *257-BDC.*" The car blares on its horn several times in quick succession, as if the driver has just discovered that it exists. He takes it back—they're *worse* than his sister, even when she was getting her permit and no one but Tresser was brave enough to drive with her. The car's wheels screech again. "Cassie, any day now."

"Okay, I've got it," Cassandra says at last (ignoring Tresser's sigh of relief). "Two people in the vehicle, both adult males. Driver...I'd say, in his mid-to-late twenties, narrow face, light eyes, brown hair. Looks serious. He's saying something, but don't ask me what..."

Tresser nods, eyes focusing on the silhouette of the driver's head. It's all he can make out, but he's glad to know what he's dealing with. "Physique?"

"On the slender side but looks powerful. The passenger is built a lot sturdier—he's about the same age, dark eyes, tan skin...a strong face. White teeth."

"Is he going to bite me? I don't need to know about his teeth."

"Let me do my job, or you *will* need to know another psychic," Cassandra retorts. Tresser shuts his mouth. "He's got broad shoulders, a lot of power in his frame. He seems...it seems like he's deferring to the driver a bit, though, I'm getting the sense that they're—yeah, the driver is the guy in charge."

"Good to know." Tresser realizes at once he has no clue where this road leads. For all he knows, he could be driving out of the city entirely, and deep within the forest. Being separated from civilization is not an idea he's fond of. "Okay, can you get me anything they're saying? Any idea where they're going?"

"Hmm...I can't tell...the passenger is looking in his rearview mirror a lot. He knows they're being followed."

Shoot. There goes the element of surprise. Pressing his phone between his ear and shoulder, Tresser slips his gun from the holster at his thigh. "He's pointed it out now," Cassandra says. "He's...laughing."

Of course he would be laughing, because demons are smug bastards. "What's the other guy doing?"

"He's driving. Not taking his eyes off the road. Seems like he knows what he's doing."

The car swerves, speeds up, then jerkily decelerates. "He doesn't. What's he saying?"

"I don't know, I can't hear—" Cassandra says; and then, "Oh."

Oh, rarely means anything good. Tresser feels the small knot of anticipation in his stomach grow tighter. "What's 'oh'?"

"Well, he's gone. The passenger is gone."

"Oh," says Tresser. Then, "Gone? Like, he just vanished?"

"Unless he jumped out of the car."

Tresser likes to think he would have noticed. "Oh," he says again. An icy chill of excitement runs along his skin. The realization they might not be dealing with normal demons is both thrilling and disorienting.

He's never faced a demon who has taken a settled form before. Only demons who have been summoned and contracted are able to do that. Contracted demons are both more powerful and more unpredictable. What's more, if these demons are settled instead of possessing a human, that means someone has *brought* them here.

"What about the driver?" he asks, realizing that he needs to make his move sooner than he thought. "What's he doing now?"

"Looking at you in his rearview mirror."

Tresser narrows his eyes at the car. Where the passenger's head once was visible, there is now nothing but empty air. The rearview mirror flashes, though he can't make out the demon's face. There's no doubt he's being watched. He curses to himself as the Jeep begins to decelerate further. There's no way it's just shitty driving anymore. He's going to have to stop in the middle of a deserted rural road at night to confront a demon.

He takes another long sip from his flask, relishing the burn of alcohol down his throat. "Can you see if he's armed or anything?" he asks, half hopeful, until Cassandra makes a negative sound.

"No clue. Sorry."

"That's okay, that's just fine. You know what, I've gotta go." Just as a precaution, he reaches into the passenger's seat and grabs his fake police badge. His gun is safe at his side. If this is going to turn into a confrontation, he will be prepared. The car in front of him rolls to a full stop and goes still, not a hint of movement to suggest life. Behind it, Tresser does the same.

"Please don't get yourself killed," Cassandra says. Then, as an afterthought, "Or if you do, don't bother me afterwards."

Tresser rolls his eyes. "Thanks for the help."

"I'm sure the Tresser Corporation is very grateful."

Tresser can't help but chuckle, even as he takes another drink. "Incredibly."

He hangs up before his conversation with Cassandra can be overheard. The last thing he needs is for this demon to know he's got friends. The hearse idles as he steps out into the darkness. His boots crunch against the ground, crushing things he can't see. He only has eyes for the car stopped just feet away with its engine still running, a beacon of light in the middle of this dark road.

He takes his time stepping up to the driver's window. When he gets there, he taps twice. The window creeps down. "Hiya. Rhode Island State Police," he says, flashing his counterfeit badge. "Sir, are you aware that your taillight is out?"

(His taillight isn't out. Tresser is counting on the demon not knowing enough about cars to know what a taillight *is.*)

The man behind the wheel of the car matches Cassandra's description to a tee. What strikes Tresser most about the man, besides the obvious suspicion in his gaze, is the guarded expression he wears. It is neither relaxed nor cocky; he may not know what Tresser wants, but he is giving nothing of his own motives away. He studies Tresser for a moment, solemn eyes scrolling over him, before he tilts his head.

"You've been following my car for fifteen minutes," he says in a low voice, smooth like waves against a sandy shore. "You haven't flashed any lights of your own. Now you're pulling me over because the lights at the back of *my* car are off?"

"That's right."

"Except they're not. My lights *can't* be off. Otherwise you wouldn't have been able to follow me."

Realization hits Tresser like a smack to the head, and for a second, he falters. Granted, that excuse was pretty weak, but now he just sounds *dumb*. He counted on his subject being stupid, or at least ignorant. There was his mistake.

Instead of backtracking, however, he presses forward with all the recklessness of someone with the bare bones of a plan and nothing to lose. He clicks his tongue, shaking his head at the man's words. "Talking back to an officer, I see. Sir, I'm going to need you to step out of the car."

"You don't want to ask for my license?" The demon sounds unimpressed.

"Step out of the car, please," Tresser emphasizes. His hand is on his hip, the hilt of his rock salt loaded gun clenched in one hand. For a tense moment, the demon does not move. Tresser's heart pounds in his ears; he counts every second of silence by the sound of his own breathing.

Then the man gives a casual shrug, and his car door clicks open. "All right."

Chapter Two

THE HUMAN STANDS about an inch taller than him. It is hardly noticeable, but to a military mind trained to pick up details, he can't miss it. It's not just his height that lets him make an impression. He is rumpled, but handsome in spite of it, with mussed golden hair and green eyes that shine even in the darkness. The human holds himself with confidence, relaxed and unconcerned. It's not the air of a dictator or a leader, but that of someone who is sure he has the upper hand, even when the cards are stacked against him.

Immediately, Nathan knows that he's dealing with an arrogant man.

Arrogant men are easy. He's dealt with enough them in the military to know how they work and how to get around them. Arrogant men are no threat to him.

Arrogant humans, even less so.

Nathan pulls himself to his full height. Unintimidated, the stranger takes a step forward. His hand is still on the holster of his gun as he gestures to the back of the car. "You really think your taillight isn't busted? Show me."

Nathan observes every detail of his posture, every minute twitch that gives him away. The man lacks subtlety. He is coiled, like a snake ready to pounce. Tension thrums beneath his relaxed demeanor. He is prepared for a fight, even if he has to start it.

"Okay," Nathan agrees, and turns his back.

That's what the human was waiting for.

Nathan feels the blow connect with his knees, and he staggers. Rather than falling, however, he reels back and rams a forceful punch into the side of the faux-cop's jaw. He goes down and Nathan follows, leaping on him and pinning him before he can even start to recover.

The human's hand scrambles for his gun. He just manages to grasp the hilt before sharp nails lock around his wrist and dig in, forcing his hand to go limp. A pained yell tears from his throat.

Nathan leans down, close enough that the human can feel his hot breath against his face. He feels the liquid sensation of his eyes switching from their human guise to natural pitch black, and the world around him sharpens. He can take in every inch of the human's face, in all its sharp, disgruntled clarity.

"Who are you?" he demands. "And what do you want from me?"

The human bares his teeth. It could almost be a smile, but there is lethal venom behind it. He looks like a proper demon.

Nathan knows he has him pinned, but the human's cleverness takes him by surprise. His leg seems to draw into him; when Nathan shifts his weight to accommodate the change, the human moves. Using the momentum of the one leg tucked beneath him, he bucks up. It's not much, but it throws Nathan off balance, and that's all the human needs to turn the fight on him.

Strong hands lock around Nathan's shoulders and squeeze. The settled form he's taken is strong, but still bruises as easily as fragile human skin. He hisses and moves to strike the human but is too slow. In a second, the human forces himself up and gets his arms around Nathan's torso.

Nathan thrashes against his arms, kicking and rebelling against his grip. A harsh fist to the face stuns him; another knocks him to the ground. In the next second, the human is on top of *him*, pinning Nathan to the ground with merciless force.

"I'm with the guy they send to deal with things like you," he snarls in the demon's grimacing face.

Nathan manages to raise an eyebrow. "Things like me?"

"Demons. There's an infestation around here, unless you haven't noticed."

"Believe me, I've noticed."

The human smirks, and maybe that's what really gets under Nathan's skin.

He has rules. He had to, coming here; demons do not enter the human world without considering the consequences first. He swore to himself that he would not use any demonic abilities unless it was necessary—and certainly not on humans.

Nathan's a man of his word, but in this case, it's *a little bit* necessary.

He doesn't want to think about what it feels like for the human. For Nathan, it is as easily as exhaling all the air in his lungs at once. It leaves him in a rush of tension, light pulsing out of him as if some invisible floodgate has been opened. He feels the rays force the human back, sending him tumbling away, stunned and disoriented. Still pulsing with the sheer raw power of energy, Nathan makes his way over to the human scrambling in the dirt and immobilizes him.

When the last of the energy fades and the human is able to see the world around him again, he seems very displeased to find a demon sitting on top of him.

"Really?"

"Really," Nathan confirms, shifting. The human's chest is hard and uncomfortable.

"That light thing, you know—that's a new one."

"Think twice before picking a fight with a High Demon," Nathan advises, forcing his voice to remain pleasant. "Did that hurt?"

It clearly hurt a lot. "A bit."

"That's not even half of what I can do. So." Leaning close, close enough that all the human can see is the black of his eyes, Nathan raises an expectant eyebrow. "Who sent you?"

For a moment, the human blinks, his mind struggling to make out what the demon is asking of him. When it dawns on him, he only grows even more annoyed. "The Tresser Corporation," he grunts out, and winds up choking when the weight on top of him shifts without warning.

Nathan hastily leans back from the human's chest, lightening the pressure there, and waits until he has stopped gasping to speak. "You're with the Tresser Corporation?" he demands. The human gives another weak cough, though it seems like it's more for appearance's sake, before nodding.

"My name's David Tresser, if that tells you anything."

Well, it tells him a bit. Nathan studies the human, eyes narrowed, taking in every inch of his rumpled appearance. He knows about the Tresser Corporation. Every high-level demon does; they're the organization responsible for maintaining relations between human and demonkind. They protect the human world against any supernatural harm... so naturally they've crossed paths with demons at some point. Demons are *always* causing trouble.

Tresser Corps agents are suave, polished, diplomatic. They're by-the-book fighters and trained spies.

The man beneath him is none of these things. As far as Nathan knows, Tresser Corps agents don't wear worn out denim jackets and drive around in hearses; they don't smile with blood in their teeth, or muss unruly hair up further. The man beneath him seems the most unlikely Tresser Corps agent in the world—let alone a Tresser himself.

When Nathan still looks like he doesn't believe him, the human huffs and gestures towards his pocket. "My driver's license and my work card. If that doesn't prove it, you can call my father. He'll be thrilled to hear from you— he keeps saying I don't know how to make friends."

Very carefully, his eyes never leaving the human's, Nathan pats down his pocket; then, reaching in, he withdraws his wallet. His gaze flickers off him just long enough to scan over his identification before he casually closes and returns it to where he found it.

"Why did you attack me?"

"What's a High Demon doing on earth in the first place?" Tresser demands. "Don't you have your own war to fight downstairs?"

"Sounds to me like you've been having troubles of your own," Nathan replies, slowly easing off of Tresser's body. If he is a Tresser Corps agent, he isn't a threat; the Corps are not their enemy. If anything, perhaps David Tresser can be a potential ally. The Corps and demons have been known to work together on occasion, and now certainly seems like a time when both sides need help.

He doesn't have many diplomatic skills, but Nathan puts the limits of what he does have to the test. He sinks low in a respectful bow before straightening up, meeting Tresser's eyes. "I represent the Demoniac Alliance, Quadrant Nine, Unit X. We've been dispatched to the human world to deal with the invaders of the Righteous Legion. They're the ones tearing your city apart; I'm one of the guys here to stop them. Our orders specified we should consider any agents of the Tresser Corporation allies."

"Sounds good to me." Finally able to move his limbs, Tresser winces as his bones creak in protest. Nathan feels a flash of sympathy, but not guilt. He was attacked first and reacted. The only thing he feels bad about is using his powers to disable his opponent (he makes a point of doing that as little as possible). That was, perhaps, not as necessary as he thought.

Just as he's forcing himself to his feet, an unexpected hand appears in Tresser's vision. Raising his eyebrows, he looks up into Nathan's expectant face. He only hesitates for a moment before accepting the olive branch, allowing himself to be pulled up.

"Naberos, Knight of the Ninth Quadrant," Nathan introduces. Tresser will know he's telling the truth. Demons can lie about many things, but never their names. "In my settled form, I go by the name Nathan Wentworth."

"Sounds nice. Very middle-class-suburban-white-dad. A hundred percent human." Tresser nods, rubbing his shoulder. "Wish I could call it a pleasure, but I've got bruises over in places bruises shouldn't be. You pack some punch, Knight of Hell."

This actually makes Nathan smile—a faint, blink-and-you-miss-it quirk of his lips that he feels guilty for a second later. There is nothing funny about his powers hurting a helpless human being. (Then again, David Tresser proved that he was hardly helpless.)

"What do you know about the war going on in Hell?" Nathan asks. Tresser shrugs. The Tresser Corporation must have information about it but have made no move to interfere. They are content to let demons handle their own affairs, as long as it doesn't interfere with the upstairs world.

"Just the basics. Righteous Legion bad, Demoniac Alliance good. Hell's made up of nine sectors—five of them are on the good side, three are on the bad side, and one wants nothing to do with anybody. I didn't realize the war had anything to do with what's happening up here."

Nathan's lips quirk again. This was the answer he was expecting. "The war is *all* about you. The Righteous Legion wants to annex the human world. The Alliance is fighting to keep that from happening."

Tresser considers this for a moment, probably comparing it to his own intelligence. Nathan can see him file the information away in his head. "So, you're here to stop them."

"Company X is here to track down any demons who have gotten into the human world and eliminate them. I'm the commanding officer on Earth, so I'm leading the effort to track down the Legion demons, most of whom appear to be located in this town. I'm currently trying to get information on what places the Legion is concentrated, and why."

He is a little surprised by the wide smile that stretches across Tresser's face. He does not seem like the smiling type. Seeing him do so makes him look years younger, almost handsome, in an unkempt way. Tresser straightens up, and it is a moment before Nathan realizes he is trying to be charming.

"Well, Nate," he says, "I think we can really help each other out here."

Nathan raises his eyebrows. "How so?"

"You need information. I need a place to start, and manpower to back me up. Sounds like we're both after the same thing." Tresser holds out his hand, undeterred when Nathan blinks at it. "What do you say? Partners?"

Slowly, Nathan says, "I'm not the 'partner' type."

"Neither am I," Tresser replies with full confidence.

Not sure exactly what he's doing, but positive he isn't making a mistake, Nathan reaches out and seizes Tresser's hand. The human's smile is so wide, almost artificial, that it gleams in the dark.

"We're gonna make a great team," he declares; and then, almost as an afterthought, with overwrought sarcasm, "Tresser Corps thanks you for your assistance!"

THE RIDE BACK into town is quiet. Tresser makes an effort, at least, but it comes off uninspired and a little artificial. When he realizes Nathan's not biting, he sighs. "Yeah, I hate small talk too," he tells him and says nothing more for the rest of the ride.

In a way, it's a relief. Nathan is still struggling to make sense of the strange human. He knows very little about human interaction (after all, this is his first time in this world), but he can tell there is something unusual about Tresser. He was so eager to partner up with a demon. Why? They may have the same objectives, but this war is not Tresser's fight. Is he really that motivated by what Nathan could bring to the table, or does he have ulterior motives for soliciting an alliance?

Nathan cannot help but be suspicious. He knows the world of ambition well. The demonic hierarchy is filled with demons who will stab one another—literally—to reach the top. If you aren't savvy, you'll be the one with a blade between your ribs.

He realizes that Tresser is a dangerous man. He does not think he's a threat to him, however. He just isn't sure what Tresser's game *is*.

He'll figure it out, though. He always does.

Having abandoned Nathan's car in the middle of the road (the human he "acquisitioned" it from will find it, eventually, probably), they travel in Tresser's car. Nathan can't help being fascinated by Tresser's choice of vehicle. Most humans would not drive around in something so macabre. The rare moments he breaks the silence, it is usually with a question about the hearse.

"It can go up to a hundred and forty," boasts Tresser—and, when Nathan clearly doesn't get it, "miles per hour. She's a real gem. I picked her up at a used car sale."

"Humans use these things to carry bodies," Nathan says.

"Yeah!" Tresser casts a glance towards the back of the car and grins. There's nothing back there, but Nathan can't help imagining a corpse anyway. He spends the remainder of the ride with stiff shoulders, jaw clenched.

Tresser doesn't know where they're actually driving until Nathan speaks up suddenly. "Right here," he says, and Tresser grinds to a halt in front of a police station.

"Umm...here?" He surveys the sea of police cars in the lot before fixing his passenger with a skeptical gaze. "Are you sure about this, Nate?"

Nathan doesn't say anything. His gaze remains rapt upon the white, many-windowed building that houses the city's law enforcement. Every detail is clear to his sharp senses. He can hear the thrum of multiple heartbeats inside the building. He can smell old coffee, see the faces of silhouetted figures in the window. He nods once, and has his seatbelt unbuckled before Tresser has even stopped the car.

Tresser scrambles out after him, grabbing his vial of holy water off the dashboard as he goes. He jogs in Nathan's stead towards the station. "Nate—wait, hold on! We got a plan here?"

"There are demons in that building," Nathan replies calmly, not faltering. "I'm going to get them out."

"We. We're a *we* now. That's called teamwork."

"I thought you weren't a partner person."

"I'm not." Tresser sounds fantastically disgruntled but follows Nathan inside without another question.

As soon as they step through the doorway, the energy of the room shifts. Even Tresser looks uncomfortable, and not just because he's standing in a police station with a loaded gun in his pocket; he can feel it too. The atmosphere is off. The air feels heavier, clinging to Nathan's delicate human skin and choking his fragile lungs. Shadows stretch longer, darkening the room and draining the place of all light.

Nathan squares his shoulders, ignoring the chill that runs down his spine. Nothing about this is right. Then again, on this mission, *not right* is just part of the game. This place feels just like home.

"This place is pleasant," Tresser remarks lightly. "Like a funeral."

Nathan hums something that's almost agreement before the sound of yelling draws their attention to the far side of the room.

The precinct is littered with police officers, looking bored behind desks or computers, but there is only one civilian in the place—a short Asian man in a rumpled T-shirt and worn-out jeans, who is currently bouncing up and down in front of the registration desk like a rabid bunny rabbit.

"I want to speak with your supervisor, goddammit!"

The woman behind the desk chews gum in a bored, rhythmic procession. She looks monumentally bored. "He's on vacation."

"Your other supervisor!"

"He's in the hospital."

"The other guy, then!"

"He's dead."

"Well, who the hell's in charge here?"

The policewoman shrugs. "Pick someone. Is there anything else I can do for you, sir?"

The man's face is red as an inferno; he looks dangerously close to leaping across the desk and shaking the woman until her teeth rattle. He is a small human, but Nathan knows better than to underestimate him. Emotion can make anyone very powerful, and this man's energy is such a cocktail of worry and rage that it's almost overwhelming.

Instead of shaking sense into the policewoman, he slams his fist down with enough force to echo in the station. "Yeah, you can let me file a missing person's report on my damn fiancée!"

The woman's shoulders slump, as if she's been over this topic more than once before and is as fed up with it as with everything else in her life. "I already told you. We can't do that."

"I'm telling *you*, she's been missing for a month! This is the fifth missing person's report I've tried to file! Now are you bastards going to do anything about it, or—"

"Easy," Nathan says, stepping up before Tresser can warn him against it. He lays a hand on the frustrated man's shoulder, easing him back before he really can rip the woman's throat out. "What's the problem here?"

Immediately, the man rounds on him. There is an incensed flush high on his cheeks, and his eyes are wild. "These sons of bitches won't do anything to find my missing fiancée!"

Maybe he can't resist trouble, or maybe he's just a masochist, but now that Nathan is involved Tresser has to stick his head in too. "You got proof that she's missing?"

"I haven't seen her in a month," the guy repeats, as if that explains everything.

"Well, buddy, usually when a girl walks out on a guy, she's not going to show up for breakfast the next day."

"That's *not*—" the guy shouts, before he catches himself; after taking a deep breath, he continues in a lower voice, though no less passionate. "Not my Lucy. She wouldn't do that. It's not just that she hasn't been home— she hasn't been into work, hasn't contacted anybody she knows, and her phone goes straight to voicemail. Lucy isn't the type of person to up and leave without telling anybody, and never for this long. Something's happened."

When he turns back to the desk again, the anger rushes back into his voice. "So I can't understand why no one's *doing anything!*"

The officer behind the desk still looks impassive, if not a little irritated. "We don't have sufficient evidence to consider her missing."

"It's been a lot more than twenty-four hours," Tresser says, narrowing his eyes. "No contact with family or friends, no cell phone activity, no previous indication that she was leaving—" He pauses, raising an eyebrow at the frustrated man, who nods with fervor. Tresser continues, "You've got every reason to consider her missing. Why are you sleeping on this? You guys are supposed to be the police."

The officer narrows her dark eyes. "We're doing our jobs, sir."

"No," Tresser shoots back, "you're not."

Nathan is impressed by Tresser's strong reaction. He takes a step back, watching as Tresser continues to rant. "The police should be doing what they're *paid* to do, and instead you're letting a woman's disappearance go uninvestigated for a *month* while her fiancé is losing his mind worrying about her? What kind of sham are you running?"

This is obviously a personal issue, to get Tresser so incensed. Nathan can't blame him. He hates corrupt authority too.

"Thank you," the aggrieved boyfriend jumps in, clapping Tresser on the chest before rounding back on the desk. "Now, I'm telling you, okay? My name's Henry Lee. My fiancée's name is Lucy Margaret Dorsett—she's been missing for almost a month now—why aren't you writing any of this down?"

"Sir." Now that Henry's gotten more people on his side, he's attracting the attention of the rest of the station. The policewoman's demeanor switched from bored to serious in an instant. "You're going to have to leave now."

Energized by the support, however, Henry isn't about to be cowed. He slams his hands down on the countertop, creating a bang that echoes throughout the entire station. "I'm not doing anything until you help me find my fiancée!"

As his shout dies down, Nathan realizes every eye in the station is on them. Only once this dawns on him does he realize they are all pitch black.

Oh, he thinks, *we're doing this now.*

His attention spins back to the policewoman at the counter once more, who is now staring Henry down with inky wells of blackness. Tendrils of shadow writhe in the room's dark corners. The air feels musky and thick. Tresser stumbles, overwhelmed by the sudden oppressive atmosphere. One hand claps across his chest, the other reaching for the hilt of his gun.

"What the hell," breathes Henry, all of a sudden very, very quiet.

Tresser is already pulling his gun out of his pocket when he turns to Nathan and freezes.

There is no fear in Nathan's expression; there is no surprise. He expected this all along, after all. "All right," he says, and sounds almost pleased. "That's what I was waiting for."

Tresser doesn't get the chance to ask what the hell he's talking about, or even to finish pulling out his gun—because in the next second Nathan explodes in a flash of blinding light that instantly envelops the entire station.

Once again, it doesn't hurt. It never hurts. It is overwhelming only in the way he loses his grip on himself. His own sense of him drifts away. At once, he is nothing but raw power, straining out and seizing each flash of dark energy he sees by the neck. He pulls them all in, drawing each writhing mask to him, and consumes it. At once, he feels like *he* ceases to exist; he is nothing but light, and energy, and utter destruction.

When the light fades, he comes back from himself. It is like drawing to the end of a long roller coaster ride. Nathan takes a deep breath and opens his eyes.

Tresser still stands in the middle of the station, Henry at his arm. They are unharmed except for windswept hair, and identical expressions of astonishment. Papers fly through the air around the station, dislodged by an invisible gale. The entire building feels much lighter. The air is breathable, and the sensation of eyes watching their every movement has vanished. The ravenous shadows have disappeared completely, leaving nothing but light in their place.

And at least a dozen police officers are passed out all over the station.

Nathan, Tresser, and Henry are the only ones left standing. This is a bold statement, because Nathan feels more than shaky. When he turns his head, his vision swims. He can feel sweat beading on his forehead, and his skin burns. Even his legs feel a little unsteady, but he remains rooted to the spot. This is all normal. It will pass in a moment.

Speaking of passing, there's also Henry, who looks dangerously close to passing out.

"Whaaaat," says the hapless man, in a slow exhale of breath; then, picking up panic as he goes, "the *fuck* was *that?*"

"*That,*" says Nathan, "is the reason they sent me to the human world."

This is apparently all Henry needs to hear to know he wants nothing to do with anything. He takes off towards the door. Nathan is still too winded to stop him. Tresser lunges, but Henry's too quick and manages to slip past him before he can get a good grip.

He makes it all the way to the door and throws it open before he runs into a mass of writhing, pulsing shadows in vague human form. The entire station erupts into static screams.

Nathan winces, and Tresser claps his hands over his ears. Henry, too stunned to move, gapes up at the nine-foot-tall eldritch horror.

A thin groan escapes his throat, like a seal being strangled. He takes a small step back, then falters.

No one is really surprised when Henry passes out cold.

Chapter Three

MALEPHOR, SERGEANT OF the Fourth Quadrant, courier for the Demoniac Alliance, and former writhing mass of unsettled demonic energy, is a little confused. She doesn't have much experience with being on Earth, but she's pretty sure kidnapping isn't what normal humans get up to in their spare time.

"Lift his legs more. Don't let him touch my paint job," the jacket-wearing human commands, gesturing imperiously with both hands. It's easy for him to order them around, because *he's* not the one hoisting a heavy human body into the back of a vehicle. Nor does he seem willing to help.

As Malephor hefts the unconscious man's feet higher, she studies the demanding human out of the corner of her eye. The man who Knight Naberos introduced as David Tresser has scruff covering the lower part of his jaw; his golden hair is mussed, almost greasy-looking, and he wears a heavy leather jacket. Most striking is the smell of alcohol Malephor can detect on his breath. The man isn't stumbling or slurring his words, but that he's imbibed tonight is obvious.

Why would Knight Naberos ally himself with a human like this? Company X's mission was not to join forces with *any* humans—they are here to cleanse the town of the Righteous Legion's infiltrators. Naberos knows this better than anyone, so why is he running around town with this human instead of his own Sergeants?

Malephor doesn't know, but there's something about the human that unsettles her. This entire situation unsettles her, and she isn't sure how much it actually has to do with Naberos.

She's not supposed to be on Earth. There are a lot of things she *should* be doing but running around in the human world is not one of them. Malephor belongs in hell. She is a soldier; there is a war going on, and she should be down there fighting it. Malephor has no place walking around in a clumsy human form, through a mortal town drenched with demonic energy.

Only the orders of Duke Serrus tore her away from the front lines. Malephor has no idea why the Duke chose *her* to deliver intelligence when so many other couriers are better suited to the job. Malephor has never been in the human world before. She's never taken a human form. She has only been on Earth for fifteen minutes, and so far, she is unimpressed.

The little man is surprisingly heavy. "Shouldn't we wait for him to wake up?" Malephor huffs, forcing his legs into the back of the car.

"We could also wait for the police to wake up," says Tresser, "but do you really want to be the one to tell them why they're all waking up with the worst hangover of their lives and no memory of all the fun?"

"They've been possessed for *weeks*," says Naberos. "They deserve to know."

The Legion *would* target law enforcement agencies first—that they took over an entire police force doesn't surprise Malephor in the least. Frankly, she agrees with the human. She doesn't want to be around when the unpossessed officers wake up, because explaining what happened will be far too much of a hassle. Humans are always quick to jump to extremes.

"They'll be fine," Tresser assures Naberos. Though it clearly doesn't sit well on his conscience, Naberos acquiesces.

With one final push, the unconscious human slides into the back of Tresser's vehicle, and Naberos climbs in after him. "Sergeant Malephor, you'll join me," he says. Malephor obeys immediately; Naberos outranks her, and as long as they are on Earth, he is her superior officer. She may respect very little about the human world, but the demonic hierarchy is something Malephor will never question.

She slips into the car, slamming the door behind her. Immediately they are engulfed in darkness. The absence of sight kicks her other senses into overdrive, and she feels everything become more acute—from the pressure of the human leaning against her side, to the sound of the car's motor sputtering as Tresser starts it up. The sharp tang of alcohol becomes more pronounced; she traces it to a flask hidden beneath Tresser's driver's seat. There is a bitter taste in the air, some sort of cologne probably mixed with air freshener, and her foot is brushing against something plush. A pillow? Its texture is rough, and Malephor can hear the shifting of down feathers.

"One second," Tresser says from up front as he begins to drive. True to his word, a beat later the lights in the back of the car switch on, and vision floods back to Malephor once more. She finds that her foot is resting against a pillow, set up on the floor next to a sleeping bag and a pile of books. Several empty snack bags litter the floor. The seats she is crammed into alongside Naberos, with the little man sandwiched between them, are made of old leather that creaks beneath their combined weight.

Her lips curl at the sight. Naberos appears unfazed, save for a small quirk of his eyebrows and the way his jaw shifts. Knight Naberos has always been a difficult man to read—Malephor, who prides herself on a prompt ability to judge others, has never had an easy time figuring him out. She knows that he is a sharp leader, brave and sensible, with a stubborn streak bigger than the entire Fourth Quadrant (if he didn't, he'd never have made it to the position he now holds). He honors loyalty above all else and surrounds himself only with people he trusts.

So he must trust Tresser then. But why? Even if Malephor could see into his head, she is not sure she could understand just what Naberos is thinking bringing this disheveled human along with them.

Instead, she can only speculate. Knowing Naberos, she's sure the other man must think Tresser can be an asset to them. She does not see how this is possible.

No sooner have they started to drive than the man between them lets out a groan and shifts, head lolling forward. Malephor stares down at him, wondering if she should be concerned.

"When he sees me, will he pass out again?" she asks Naberos, who scoffs.

"Sergeant Malephor, the only reason he passed out the first time was because you appeared in your unsettled form. On Earth, our orders are to settle into human form. If you'd done that, he wouldn't have lost it in the first place."

It's not a reprimand, exactly, but Malephor knows Naberos is scolding her. She tries not to look cowed beneath her superior officer's stern gaze. In her defense, she never *received* the order to settle. Duke Serrus told her to deliver the intelligence to Naberos—that's all. This abduction has complicated her entire mission, when she really should have been back already. Now she's stuck in this heavy-limbed human form which won't move the way she wants it to, and complicit in a kidnapping.

Saying any of this to Naberos, she knows, would be useless. "I apologize, Sir," she says instead, bowing her head. The show of deference is enough for Naberos, who nods and turns his attention to the stirring human.

"Henry?" he prompts in a low voice, shaking the human by the shoulder. "It's all right. You just fainted."

"Fainted?" The human's voice comes out groggy and rough. "You're kidding me..."

When he lifts his head, drooping eyes suddenly go wide. Astonishment clouds his face as his gaze swivels from one end of the car to the other, taking in everything from Tresser driving to the two men keeping him in place.

Malephor can see the exact moment everything comes rushing back to him. She feels it too, because Henry jerks upwards, and nearly topples over as the car hits a speed bump.

"What the hell," he exclaims, panic causing his voice to break, "what the *hell,* what the holy hell was *that?* You—" He gapes at Naberos, fumbling over his own tongue. "What even *are* you? And those cops, what were *they?* What the hell is going on—and where are we *going?*"

"We've abducted you," Malephor says promptly, because it's true. Naberos shoots her a sharp look. It might not have been the best thing to say.

When Henry lets out another sputter and tries to jump to his feet again, Naberos grabs his arm to hold him still. "It's okay. We just want to talk."

"Okay, fine," Henry exclaims, still several shades of freaking out. *"Talk.* What are you supposed to be, some kind of demon?"

Huh. He's either very sharp, or good at guessing. Naberos's composure is remarkable. "You got it, actually," he replies, voice level in a way that is probably meant to soothe the frightened man. "My name is Nathan Wentworth. Up front is David Tresser, and the entity next to you is a demon known as Malephor. We're trying to free this town of chaotic influence caused by a group of evil demons out to destroy mankind. Those were what was in the police station, and when I cleansed them, I destroyed the demons controlling them. We took you with us to make sure that you were okay."

Henry stares at him for a very long moment, face blank. Naberos meets his gaze for as long as it takes to get uncomfortable, before he clears his throat. Slowly, Henry raises a hand and pinches himself in the cheek. When this fails to have the desired effect (whatever he was going for—Malephor doesn't know, humans are weird) he buries a hand in his hair and lets out a high-pitched laugh.

"You're kidding," he says, looking at Naberos with a pleading expression. "You're...joking, right?"

"You wish," calls Tresser from the front. Naberos purses his lips, though whether this is in response to Henry's question or Tresser's flippancy is anyone's guess.

"I know this is a lot to take in."

"A lot?" Henry demands and laughs again. When he turns to Malephor, he looks accusatory, and she goes stiff in defense. "So you were the freaky black shadow thing?"

"I was."

"Oh my god." Henry buries his head in his hands, still laughing softly. He doesn't move for a very long time.

After a few minutes—when it's become apparent that Henry isn't going to rejoin the bizarre scene anytime soon—Tresser calls out from the front, "Nate, we could just drop him off on the side of the road somewhere. And, like, leave him. He'll be fine."

In Malephor's opinion, this seems like a very good idea. Naberos, however, frowns and shakes his head. His hand is still on Henry's back, and he's massaging up and down as if he's not sure what he should be doing but is determined to do it anyway. "We're not doing that. He's processing, Tresser. Give him a minute."

She doesn't realize that Naberos is looking at her until the Knight clears his throat. Malephor's gaze snaps back to him once more, and she is immediately at attention. "Sergeant," says Naberos, "what intelligence do you have to share?"

Finally, the point of her mission. Malephor feels a rush of relief, mingled with irritation that it's taken this long. "Duke Serrus has intelligence on the various humans who have gone missing around the site of the barrier breach. They're being held in a Grey prison somewhere deep within the Seventh Quadrant. What's being done to them there is unknown, but intelligence has picked up on various heat signatures that can only be caused by mortals."

Naberos looks as troubled as Serrus did when recounting the information to Malephor. There's no question why. No human can survive in Hell for long, even if proper life support is being provided to them. Without the ability to withstand the intense environment, humans cannot stay in hell. Any prisoners would be basically condemned, unless they were recovered as soon as possible. It may already be too late for the unfortunate prisoners.

The slew of disappearances of known magic practitioners since the Legion invaded could easily go unnoticed if no police force was there to investigate. Now, the sinister puzzle looks a lot clearer. With the pieces lining up, Naberos looks more troubled than ever.

Company X has one job on Earth—to eliminate the demonic threat. They are not responsible for the disappearances, nor for the humans coming back to life. Serrus wouldn't have given Naberos this information if he didn't think he needed it.

"Sergeant," Naberos says, looking pensive, "how many people are missing?"

The information floods from Malephor's mouth as easily as if she were hearing it the first time. Her job was to remember Serrus's information, so she didn't forget a word. "There are six confirmed abductions. Joshua O'Brien, witch; Alfred Hancock, medium; Belinda Juarez, psychic; William Grant, exorcist; Justine Phelps, psychic; and Lucy Dorsett, exorcist."

Without warning, Henry springs up like he's been shot. Startled, Naberos falls back, and even Malephor draws away at the look in the human's suddenly blazing eyes. Henry looks ravenous, furious, desperate and terrified all at once. It's a combination of emotions that Malephor has never seen before, and it frightens her. She has no clue what she could have said until Henry opens his mouth, and his words spill out in a single breath.

"Lucy? You know where Lucy is? That's her, that's *Lucy,* you just *said* you know where she is—"

"Whoa, *wait* a second," Tresser exclaims at the same time, suddenly rapt upon the conversation. "You mean those disappearances are related to all this too?"

Henry seizes Malephor by the shoulders, and the demon is too stunned to pull away. "Where the hell is Lucy?"

"How did my intelligence miss this?"

"Was she kidnapped by demons?"

"What the hell do they want with *people?*"

Through the storm, Naberos remains silent, his face clouded over, and brows furrowed in deep thought. His thoughts, as always, are locked behind the intensely private barrier of his mind, closed off even to Malephor's perceptive eye.

The only thing Malephor knows for sure is that things have just gotten a *lot* more complicated.

AND THAT'S HOW they end up adopting another human.

Malephor's mission is spiraling out of control. It was the simplest thing into the world: go into the human world, give Naberos the intelligence, come back. Except she's *not* going back, because somehow, they're discussing battle plans with a very determined Henry Lee, who has no clue what's going on but is dead-set on being a part of it anyway.

Malephor can understand, sort of. Henry loves his fiancée, so he's determined to get her back by any means possible. It's typical human sentimentality, but nothing about it is surprising. Malephor knows how easy it is for humans to fall in love and be carried away by their emotions because of it.

Demons are a different species entirely. Demons operate on logic, on necessity, functionality. Demons do not lose themselves to something as mundane as emotion. There is no place for feelings in hell, and especially no place for them in the hierarchy. In hell, everyone has their roles, and they fulfill them. Rarely, if ever, has Malephor known a demon to fall in love.

(She fights against the Righteous Legion and their xenophobic dogma, but to claim there have never been times when she's *understood* why they perceive humans as weak and contemptible would be a lie.)

She does not hate humans for this emotion. She doesn't hate Henry. She just doesn't understand him.

"This isn't your war," she says. Every head in the car turns towards her; she's kept her mouth shut for most of the conversation, so to hear her speak now takes everyone aback. Malephor doesn't falter. "Deciding to fight against something you don't understand is going to get you killed. There's no reason for you to do this."

Henry huffs out a dry laugh, without an ounce of humor. "As long as Lucy's somewhere in danger, that's all the reason I need." When he turns back to the rest of the group, he looks resolute. "As long as you're looking for her, I'm sticking with you guys."

A moment of silence follows. Tresser looks like he finds this entire situation exasperating. Meanwhile, Naberos frowns at Henry as if trying to read a secret message in his eyes. There's no way Naberos can allow this. An untrained human has no place among military ranks. Even Tresser has some field experience, so Malephor can understand why his presence is allowed, but Henry?

"All right," Naberos says. "You can help us."

The tiny flame of confidence in the sanity of this mission that had been burning in Malephor's head sputters and dies.

"All right!" Tresser claps his hands and crawls into the front of the car once more. "That settles that. We should find a place to bed down for the night, because I'm sure everyone isn't going to be able to sleep in the back of the hearse."

Wait—what? Just like that? Malephor casts an incredulous look at Naberos, who doesn't seem to notice—or, if he does, doesn't acknowledge it. This mission already seems disorganized to the extreme, especially with the new intelligence they've just been given. Adding another human to the mix feels like the worst thing they could do, and yet Naberos looks sure of himself.

Malephor trusts Naberos, as a superior officer and an intelligent man. However, she cannot see how this can possibly be a good idea.

She is a courier. She delivers messages and information. It is not her place to raise questions, just as it isn't her place to fight battles. Has that ever stopped her before?

Up front, she hears a cell phone buzzing, and Tresser's low voice answering the call. Malephor leans over Henry, ignoring the human entirely as he focuses on Naberos. She isn't questioning the Knight's order—she just needs to know what's going on here. "Sir, what is the objective of your mission?"

Naberos raises an eyebrow. "That seems obvious, doesn't it, Sergeant. Eliminate the demon threat to the human world."

Malephor knows this. She also knows why Naberos was chosen to lead this mission—she knows it as well as the entire military does, especially Naberos himself. The selection of Naberos is not just the military sending one of their best Knights on a specialized mission. They are also sending their greatest weapon.

Now Malephor cannot help but wonder if Naberos knows what he's doing, or if his confidence in his own ability is clouding his judgment. "Your orders are to capture or kill any Legion demon you find. Sir, with all due respect, why complicate this mission further?"

Naberos doesn't look fazed by the skepticism; he handles it with a cool Malephor doubts she'd be able to muster under the same scrutiny. "Right now, I have each of my sergeants leading platoons to scour the town. They know what their orders are. So do I. Sergeant Malephor, you do not have to agree with my choices, but I know what I'm doing. My judgment isn't yours to question."

Malephor presses her lips in a thin line. "Yes, sir."

"You're *what?*"

A loud exclamation from the front of the car jerks everyone's attention towards Tresser. The man is holding his phone to his ear, steering the vehicle one-handed; this is not as alarming as the fact that most of Tresser's attention seems to be on his conversation instead of the road.

Malephor focuses her hearing on the phone call and can pick up an onslaught of noise—a rush of static, the sound of things shattering, and over it all a slightly frantic voice huffing into the line. "I'm being *attacked*, and I need you here now. I don't know how long these wards will hold out."

"Cassie, what do you mean by—"

"I *mean*, a large demon has descended on my house and is trying to get in, while I'm trying everything I can think of to keep it out! And I don't know how long I can hold on here, so *please* tell me that you're on your way!"

The vehicle does an abrupt about-face that sends all three of its backseat passengers careening to the side.

Malephor's shoulder slams against the hearse door, a jolt of pain shooting through her arm. She grunts, pushing herself upright again. Henry's full weight has fallen on top of her, so Malephor has to shove the squirming human up as well, almost into Naberos's lap.

Tresser doesn't notice, or he doesn't care. Suddenly the car is speeding away from the city, tearing through the streets with abandon. It's a miracle Tresser doesn't run anyone over. He pays no attention to pedestrians or other cars, racing through the streets with a breakneck recklessness that stands a good chance of getting all of them killed. When the car lurches forward again, Malephor throws a hand out to keep Henry from toppling over and feels her frustration spike to an all-time high.

"Human, what is this?"

Tresser ignores her, instead holding his phone near his mouth in one white-knuckled hand. "On my way, Cassie," he says, before hanging up and tossing the phone onto the seat.

"Tresser!" Naberos pounds a hand on the car's divider and hauls himself up to catch a glimpse of the human's face. "Want to tell me going on?"

Where he'd been more than happy to ignore Malephor, Naberos's question actually wins a response. "Change of plans!" Tresser calls over his shoulder. "We've gotta go save a psychic!"

Naberos settles back in his seat once again, confused clear on his face. He looks as baffled as Malephor feels. When Henry glances around for seatbelts and makes a face when he sees there are none, Malephor realizes they're in for a long ride.

This is *not* what she came to Earth for.

THE MOMENT THEY pull up to Cassandra Carlyle's house, it's obvious that her call for help was necessary.

For one thing, there isn't a house there anymore.

At one time Malephor is sure Cassandra must have had a very nice house—rustic, probably, considering it's a few miles off from civilization, and cozy in the way humans tend to like their homes—but where Cassandra's domain once stood now there is only a swirling cloud of blackness. The mass of writhing, pulsing demonic energy seems to roar. Lightning flashes and rolling thunder echoes through the ominous night. The monster roils, furious, its raw power rippling through the air.

"What the hell is that?" Henry mutters, sounding faint.

Naberos's lips are pressed into a thin line. "That," he says, "is a High Demon."

A *Grey* High Demon, to be exact. A Grey High Demon in the human world, attacking Cassandra in her home— and it takes a moment of gaping for Malephor to realize that there *is* actually a house beneath that oily mass, and a *human* inside of it.

Well—maybe. If the human is still alive, which is doubtful, because the demon surrounding the house seems intent on strangling every bit of life out of it.

"That's...a demon thing," says Henry, a dazed look on his face. "Is this a normal day for you?"

"No," Naberos says, at the same time Tresser answers, "Sorta."

"Okay," Henry says, and is wise enough to leave it at that.

They're only at the top of the long driveway when the car's engine gives an awful groan and dies. Tresser spits out a curse, slapping the dashboard, then leaning forward to draw an awful wail from the horn. "Son of a bitch! Goddamn pain in the ass demon magic—"

"Tresser, enough." Naberos reaches forward, laying a hand on Tresser's shoulder and pulling him back—away from the horn, thankfully. Tresser cuts his diatribe off, continuing to sulk in the front seat, while Naberos turns to the rest of the car's occupants. "I guess this means we'll walk."

"Or run," says Henry, still staring up at the pulsing High Demon. "In the other direction."

"You can stay in the car." Naberos is halfway out the back of the hearse already. Malephor follows and is relieved by the feeling of solid ground under her feet. It only takes a second for Henry to scramble out after them.

This would be a suicide mission for any human to take on alone. There's no way Tresser could have fought this thing on his own; Cassandra, helpless inside her house, never stood a chance. The only thing keeping the demon from getting inside is a series of intricate wards designed to deter any demonic invaders. Instead of the demon being able to infiltrate her home, he's been blocked out; so he's wrapped himself around the entire house in an attempt to force Cassandra out and into his clutches.

The Greys might not be subtle, but they sure are vicious. Malephor is a little impressed by this demon's determination.

They're halfway up the driveway when Naberos suddenly stops dead in his tracks, screeching the rest of the group to a halt with him. He has realized the exact thing Malephor knew from the beginning. "Tresser, I can't go in there."

"What do you mean?"

"I mean, I can't go in that house. I can't get much closer than this. The house is warded against demons."

We're the circumstances any less urgent, Tresser would surely find this amusing. As it is, he just looks harried, though he can't help cracking a smirk anyway as he takes in the expression of utter annoyance on Naberos's face. "Aww, poor little demon can't break down a few locked doors?"

Stubborn as ever, Nathan refuses to be embarrassed. "They're very good wards."

It's true—these are some of the most powerful wards Malephor has ever encountered. From a distance it's hard to get a read each of their express purposes, let alone how to break them. The wards are *strong,* especially if they're keeping something like this out.

The only problem is that they're also keeping out the only people who stand a chance of helping Cassandra. The protections keeping her safe could be the very things that wind up getting her killed.

Narrowing her eyes, Malephor glances between the Grey demon and their small party. It's easy to see who stands the better chance of success. The Grey is massive and powerful. Up against him, Naberos is at a disadvantage. He's inexperienced at dealing with wards, and after the scene at the police station, he is not at full strength. If Naberos went up against this demon, he could easily lose.

Malephor has no such limitations.

Here's the thing about couriers: they receive very specialized training and are expected to master it. A courier's job is to get information from one demon to another, no matter where they are or what stands in their way. Be it unfriendly weather, entire worlds between them...or wards.

Couriers are very good at breaking wards.

One thing couriers are not trained to do is fight. The battlefield is no place for a messenger. They stay in the background, zipping vital information back and forth, and that's their place. Malephor has grown up knowing it…

But she has never been satisfied.

Right now, there is a conflict in front of her. She has an objective; she has an enemy. It's a job to do, just like any message she's ever run. Malephor shoves all remaining thoughts of chance outcomes from her head as her focus zeroes in on the one thing in front of her: a battle to win.

She charges ahead of Naberos and the rest of the group, heedless of whether or not they choose to follow. Her attention is locked on the demon. As she moves, she can feel the adrenaline course through her human body, sparking her to life. Her limbs vibrate with power; her vision fades to black and red, picking up every twitch, every near-imperceptible movement. She can hear the rush of blood through her veins. If she had a heart, it would be pounding like a war drum.

Malephor can feel the wards trying to push her back the closer she gets, but she charges right through them. Where other demons would struggle and falter under the magic pushing her back, Malephor uses the energy to charge her war-ready limbs.

She hears the shriek of the Grey in her ears, sneering at her approach. *You are small and weak. The human is mine.*

Not as long as Malephor is here to protect her, she isn't.

She is a messenger, but she is also a warrior. War is what she was born for. She has known this all her life and trained relentlessly to match the most hardened enemy. If she has to take on a High Demon to get her taste of blood, so be it. A true warrior is never defeated.

You are weak, the Grey declares again, causing the air around him to ripple with shock waves strong enough to knock any human unconscious. *You cannot touch me.*

Malephor doesn't have to.

She waits until she can feel the full force of the ward's repel—a harsh push, determined to keep her away by any means necessary—and lets it fling her backwards. She arches in the air and catches herself against the nearest massive tree in an effortless crouch. Narrowing her eyes at the Grey, she heaves her weight forward and *pulls.*

A crack seems to shake the earth. Malephor hauls the massive tree trunk above her head, ignoring the well in the ground left behind. Her muscles strain beneath the weight; a shower of dirt rains down upon her head. Rage twists her face into a ravenous grimace. She grits her teeth, and throws.

The tree does not hit Cassandra's house, though it is directly in its path. Instead, it bounces off the demon engulfing it, like a truck hitting a steel wall head-on. The Grey lets out an incensed wail as the tree tears a hole straight through his black mass. Through the gaping wound, Malephor can make out a window framed by painted shutters. It almost glows in the sea of blackness, and Malephor spots a tiny human face gaping out at her. Then the Grey shudders, causing the house to rock with him, and the human vanishes from view.

The Grey bellows with rage and pulls away from the house at last, drawing himself up to his full height. He towers to the tops of the tallest trees, staring down at Malephor like a child ready to stomp on a bug. The writhing mass of shadow has taken on a vague human form and takes one step forward away from Cassandra's house.

This is all the opening Malephor needs.

She never remembers a fight. Training takes over. Instinct propels her on, keeping her from losing her life to the distraction of thinking. There is no room for emotion in the middle of a battle—no room for fear, for sorrow, for disbelief. There is only your enemy, and you. Malephor throws herself into her attack with a great burst of power and abandon, and that is all she knows.

She sees herself attack the demon, blasting it with wave after wave of raw force. She feels each explosion as it pulses out of her body. Her bones creak and organs compress with each new attack by the Grey. The massive shadow stumbles, sways, swinging his arms in a furious attempt to fight her back. Malephor watches the shreds of shadow tear off and disintegrate. The High Demon's body literally eats away at itself beneath the continuous assault of energy.

She hears the bone-shattering roar as the Grey finally arches backwards in agony. With one final explosion that rocks the forest, it vanishes. Ash rains down from the black sky; the last of the lightning fades away. Malephor falls to her knees in the wreckage of the storm she has created.

The forest is silent. The world is empty. Though completely spent, Malephor is victorious. Never in her life has such power coursed through her veins, thrumming like raw energy underneath the clunky tarp of human skin.

A few seconds seem to drag on for centuries before footsteps above her let him know that she is no longer alone. She cracks her eyes open to see Naberos gaping down at her, not bothering to hide the shock on his face.

"It was harder than it looked," is all Malephor says.

Naberos is silent for a long moment before holding out a hand. Malephor takes it, accepting the help as she hauls herself back to her feet. "Don't know how you did that—but well done, Sergeant," Naberos says. For the first time, Malephor can hear the respect in his tone. From the normally reticent Knight, this approval sends a rush of surprise through her system. It is quickly replaced by pride.

Henry stares at her, mouth hanging open shamelessly. "Remind me not to piss you off."

"Doubt it would do any good," Malephor replies, and as she speaks, she realizes she's grinning.

The sound of a door being thrown open calls their attention back to the house—and to Tresser, who is standing on the front porch and ready to greet Cassandra when the woman rushes out. Cassandra's breathing is heavy; her skin is pale, face lined with sweat. She looks like she's just survived the end of the world. The first thing she does is throw her arms around Tresser, squeezing him in silent thanks. Tresser lowers his head and murmurs something. Cassandra manages to nod.

Then she pulls away and turns to the remaining rescuers. They are all strangers to her, but she does not seem to care. She takes a deep breath and then gives a smile that has Malephor's wild mane of hair standing on end as if she's been struck by lightning.

"Well, that was exciting, wasn't it? How about you all come inside!"

Cassandra turns that mild gaze on Malephor and directs the full force of her relieved grin towards her.

Suddenly Malephor feels like she could battle a hundred High Demons.

Cassandra Carlyle, she decides, is very different from a normal human.

GRANTED, SHE'S NEVER met a human before today.

Malephor, like all demons, *knows of* humans. She studied them in her youth; and during her time spent guarding the barrier before the war, she witnessed many comrades pass through and return with tales to tell. All she's ever learned about humans has only affirmed her belief that they are different. They do not think like demons, live like demons, feel like demons.

Malephor grew up in the Fourth Quadrant—which, while officially part of the Demoniac Alliance, saw many soldiers leave to join the Legion when war broke out. The environment she grew up in did little to dissuade her of her conceptions of humanity. While she's never gone so far as to declare them lesser, she took for granted that she could never respect a human.

Cassandra Carlyle has an oversized ponytail of sandy curls and large bright eyes. She dresses in sunshine colors and oversized jewelry. In her house, she prefers to go barefoot, and encourages her guests to do the same. Everything about her appearance seems to raise its voice, calling for attention, for *something*. Despite this, she is quiet and unassuming. She demands nothing from anyone, least of all respect. She wins it from Malephor the moment she invites them into her home.

Cassandra is not a witch, but the wards around her house are so carefully crafted that the demons can only enter on Cassandra's invitation. Once she has the entire group seated in her warmly lit living room, she is quick to make sure everyone is comfortable and unharmed. Then, she busies herself passing out refreshments to anyone who wants them. Naberos and Henry get water; Tresser and Malephor get tea.

Malephor has never had human food before. The taste of tea is sharp and rich in her mouth, causing her to splutter. She lurches forward, barely managing to avoid spilling the drink everywhere, and when she regains her composure, she finds Cassandra peering at her.

"Are you okay?" she asks, an edge of worry in her voice. "If it's too strong, I could get you water instead. Or juice? I'm sure we have some sort of juice..."

She's *genuinely* concerned about her, Malephor realizes with a jolt. She draws the tea closer to her chest. "It's fine," she replies tonelessly. "Great."

Cassandra smiles at her. She doesn't mean to, but Malephor feels her own lips quirk up in response.

"*Wow*. That's the first time I've ever seen you smile!"

She isn't sure what her face looks like when she turns to Henry, but it's enough to make the man scramble backward, nearly winding up in Naberos's lap in his haste to get away. Naberos just pats Henry on the head and nudges him over.

Tresser explained very little about Cassandra in the car, but it was enough for Malephor to know the basics. Cassandra is a psychic, a medium, and an associate of the Tresser Corporation. Her specialties are energy work and communicating with the dead. She also enjoys nature enough to live outside of the city, has a really nice interior decorating style, and makes a mean cup of tea. Tresser didn't tell Malephor any of *that*; she's figured it out herself.

As long as she's on Earth, Malephor decides she wants to learn more about Cassandra Carlyle. For the experience of getting to know a human, if nothing else (Henry and Tresser don't count). Malephor wants to know as much as she can about Cassandra.

Now Cassandra has her head bowed and is discussing something with Tresser and Naberos in a low voice. Henry is unsubtly trying to eavesdrop; Malephor is busy studying the way Cassandra's brows knit together when she frowns.

When Naberos addresses her by name, she is jerked back to the present like a car veering off the road. She jolts up, eyes wide, and tries to ignore Naberos's raised eyebrow.

"Sergeant," he says. "I was going to ask if you think this could be another kidnapping attempt."

"Definitely, sir," she replies without hesitation. If the Greys were going around abducting humans, it would require lots of power and the element of surprise. A High Demon ambushing Cassandra in her home at night is the perfect example. Cassandra's wards were the only thing that saved her. If there is a next time, she might not be so lucky. The thought of this woman being dragged down to Hell makes something in Malephor's stomach feel tight.

Naberos turns back to Cassandra, who has a frown set on her face. "We'll go to every length to keep you safe," Naberos promises solemnly. "You're under the protection of both the Demoniac Alliance and the Tresser Corporation. I'll assign a sentry to you to protect you in case you should be attacked again."

"I would appreciate that, sir," says Cassandra.

"Sergeant Malephor. You will stay by Cassandra's side and protect her from all threats until our mission is complete."

Malephor's spine stiffens. She stares at Naberos, cool and unreactive. This is not her mission. "With all respect, sir," she says, "but my orders were to return to hell."

"Sure. That was before you took on a High Demon by yourself and *won,*" Naberos replies, one eyebrow raised. Malephor tries not to react beneath his gaze. She knows what a feat she's pulled off. Defeating a powerful High Demon is almost unheard of for a lesser demon, but Malephor has not spent her life training in secret as a warrior for nothing. She has always been confident in her own abilities, but tonight was the first time they were put to the ultimate test.

She won, but her victory might now have consequences she couldn't have predicted. "Your new orders," Naberos says, "are to stay in the human world and protect Cassandra. We need all hands on deck, Sergeant. You're needed here more than down there."

Her first instinct is to protest. Every inch of her wants to be back in the thick of war. Hell is where she belongs. Earth, with its strange customs and incomprehensible people, is not her place. She needs to fight to defend her own world.

Logic, however, forces its way through the cracks in her resolve. Her victory against the Grey means she qualifies to be promoted in rank to a High Demon herself. Naberos can recommend her for that; if Malephor fulfills these new orders, that recommendation is assured.

Also, staying on Earth has other benefits. It means staying in the thick of a potential fight. It means no longer being considered, "just a messenger". And it means staying with Cassandra.

She finds herself nodding before she can think too hard about what she's giving up. "Yes, sir. I understand."

Naberos smiles. "Thank you, Sergeant."

Henry clears his throat, breaking any remaining tension. "Not to be pushy, but... I'm gonna be pushy. If you're a psychic, does that mean you can find Lucy?"

Cassandra purses her lips, bracing elbows against her knees, and nods. "First thing tomorrow, I'll see what I can divine. I'll try scrying, and I should be able to see what happened to her."

The look of relief that passes across Henry's face is impossible to ignore. He relaxes into the couch, looking as if a great weight has just been lifted from his shoulders.

"In that case, Cassie," Tresser says, "you got some beds for tonight? It's late, and we're going to have a long day tomorrow."

"I have a guest room." Cassandra rises to her feet and surveys the assembly of people on the couch. Her lips purse in deliberation before she nods to herself. "You two," she says, gesturing to Tresser and Naberos, "can share the guest room." She then turns to Malephor and Henry. "The couch is comfortable enough, but I have pillows and blankets in case you'd rather sleep on the floor."

Naberos opens his mouth, ready to give up his spot in the bed to someone else, but Tresser spots this and clamps a hand around his arm before he gets the chance. "Great, Cassie! Thanks a lot!"

"Tresser—"

Naberos and Tresser rise to their feet, and Tresser mutters something to Naberos that causes his protest to die in his throat. No longer squeezed tight on the couch, Henry sighs and stretches himself out. An approving noise escapes his throat as he shifts around to feel out the softness of the pillows.

Malephor, on the other hand, decides she'd rather take the floor than share a couch with Henry. The human looks like an active sleeper, and the last thing she needs is to wake up in the middle of the night to find Henry's elbow in her ribs or his foot in her face. She slides to the floor. The carpet is soft beneath her, which is a relief—she will not be sleeping on hard wood.

"So, where's the guest room?" Tresser asks cheerfully. Anything, Malephor supposes, would be better than sleeping in the back of a hearse.

"Oh, George can show you the way."

George, Malephor assumes, would be the ghost in Cassandra's house. She was conscious of his presence ever since she stepped through the door, but figured Cassandra knew of him and thus deemed him safe. Naberos doesn't seem surprised by the mention of George either, but Henry lifts his head with a frown and Tresser's eyebrows raise.

"George would be...your pet ghost?"

Cassandra sighs. Naberos fixes a stern glare on Tresser, who doesn't bother responding. His dark eyes are darting around the room, suddenly bright with paranoia. He scans the air around him as if he'll be able to see the undead figure lounging on the nearest chair. It only takes a few seconds for realization to dawn.

"You're afraid of ghosts?" Naberos looks delighted.

"I'm not—*not* afraid of ghosts," Tresser insists, but his words fumble over one another. "They're just not something I deal with. I can handle demons, fine. Living people, most of them are awful, but whatever. Ghosts aren't my jurisdiction."

Henry tilts his head, trying to look sympathetic though he's clearly fighting off a laugh. "Let me guess— you had a bad childhood experience?"

"Shut up, or we'll let the ghost have you."

As if this idea agrees with George, all the lights in the room suddenly flicker. They go dark for one second. The next finds Tresser half in Naberos's arms, eyes wide, lips curled in a battle-ready grimace. Naberos steadies him with an arm around his waist, looking tolerant, if a little bewildered.

Malephor misses hell.

Then Cassandra crouches in front of her and offers a smile that makes Malephor's entire body feel lighter all at once. "I'll go dig up those blankets," she says, and Malephor stares at her for a few seconds before remembering to nod.

If she has to stay on Earth for the time being, she can't think of anywhere she'd rather be than here. It isn't her original assignment, but protecting Cassandra feels like it will be the most important mission she's ever received.

Chapter Four

BY NOW, HENRY has figured out he's in over his head.

A lot of things in the past twelve hours have made this *really* freaking obvious. The giant black cloud that ate Cassandra's house, for one thing. That was the freakiest thing he's ever seen, even freakier than the police station straight out of the uncanny valley. He's had a lot of nightmares (especially since Lucy went missing) but he never could have dreamed that up.

Now he's fighting some sort of war with a couple of demons and an alcoholic homeless bounty hunter. (When he called Tresser this, he got a really pinched look on his face, laughed loudly, and took a long sip from his flask). He's on a quest to find his missing fiancée, who's apparently been kidnapped and dragged to Hell. Like, actual Hell. By demons. And the only way to save her is to team up with more demons.

Henry is way out of his depth here.

Still, it doesn't *really* hit him until he's sitting around a table in Cassandra Carlyle's warm, sunlight kitchen, with eggs and bacon in front of him, a vase of wildflowers to his right, and Tresser the Homeless Bounty Hunter on his left.

Life has really gotten weird since Lucy vanished, but this...this takes the cake. Heck, it takes the whole damn bakery.

Cassandra was insistent upon them eating breakfast, and even more insistent upon cooking it herself. Malephor refused to leave her side to join them; she justified this by asserting that demons do not have to eat in their settled forms. This hasn't stopped Nathan from picking up a healthy serving of bacon.

He scarfs it down like a starving man who hasn't seen food in years. When he catches his tablemates gawking at him, he barely slows. "Human food is amazing," he gushes, remarkable, considering he's very much not the gushing type. "It's so much better than what we have in Hell. It's like...pure ecstasy."

"That's a good way to describe bacon," agrees Henry.

Nathan shovels more food into his mouth. Wordlessly, Tresser picks up a few pieces of bacon from his plate and transfers them to the demon's.

It's obvious that Tresser has more tact than Henry's first impression of him implied, because he waits until they're almost done with eating to ask the question Henry knows he's been dying to bring up. To be fair, so has he. There are a lot of things that are easy to forget in lieu of bigger things, like a demon almost swallowing a house. This is not one of them.

"So, you wanna explain what the heck that was last night? You know, in the police station, with the whole, 'vroooom, zim zam, demons are dead' thing. That was an exorcism like I've never seen."

Nathan goes very still. This wasn't a topic he wanted brought up, and it couldn't be more obvious; but, well, it's here now. There's no escaping it, no lying, no talking his way around it. Tresser and Henry both saw what happened last night. Nathan went full Psychic Rambo on over a dozen demons, and if Tresser's reaction is any clue, this is not a normal thing.

"It wasn't an exorcism," Nathan finally says, "Not really."

Henry leans forward. Every shred of common sense he possesses is telling him to let demon business *stay* demon business—but god knows he's never been good at keeping his mouth shut.

"Well?" he presses. "What was it?"

Nathan frowns down at his plate for seconds that drag on like hours; when he finally sighs, it is a relief for everyone. "Those were my powers," he explains. "Every demon has their own set of abilities, that they can utilize however they want. Some shapeshift, others control the electricity or nature. My ability is a bit more complex. I'm able to channel, manipulate, and absorb demonic energy."

His words settle over the table like a heavy blanket. The lump of breakfast on Henry's tongue suddenly tastes bland. His eyes swivel to Tresser for help, but he's just staring at Nathan with something close to incredulity.

"You're kidding me," he mumbles. "That's...freaking amazing."

Uncomfortable, Nathan shrugs. "It's just what I can do. Believe me, other demons view it as more of a threat than a talent—and see me the same way."

"Okay, but still amazing. The people who don't like it can screw off," Tresser amends. Nathan's lips press into a thin line, and Henry can't tell if he's pleased or embarrassed by such bluntness.

All he knows is that he's still lost. He clears his throat. "Umm, hello? Clue me in here. Demonic energy is...energy from demons?

"Wow. You're the sharpest knife in the drawer," chimes Tresser. Nathan rolls his eyes, and from the way Tresser jolts, he definitely gets kicked under the table.

"Everything's got energy. Think of demonic energy as…an invisible black cloud of oil that spills on anyone and anything it touches. It tends to be negative, and is very, very powerful. Too much of it in one place can bring forth an actual demon; and of course, demons themselves are made of it."

Henry swallows. It's still hard to hear someone talk about "demons" so frankly and not think it's a joke. He's half expecting one of them to slap the table and burst out with a laughing "gotcha!" at any second.

He waits. It doesn't happen. He exhales in a great huff and takes a sip of his orange juice. It would be good if there were something a little stronger in it; as it is, Henry can cope. "So, it's like if all humans had powers. Right?" he asks once he's collected himself again. His tablemates don't seem to know where he's going but nod all the same. "They can do all this cool stuff. And then there's this one guy who controls blood. Like, that's his power. Just. Blood. He sucks it out, he moves it around, he makes it disappear while it's inside you. Is that it?"

Tresser looks queasy; Nathan isn't fazed a bit. "Basically."

"Damn," Henry mutters. "I would *hate* that guy."

"*Interitus,*" Nathan mumbles. When everyone looks up at him, his gaze swivels back down to his plate. "That's what I'm called, I mean, back home."

"Okay, so you get a cool nickname out of it." Henry chomps down on a piece of bacon. "And people call you a Knight too. Anything else we should know about your role in World War Demon?"

A throat clears behind him. Henry freezes up. There's no mistaking *that* sound.

"Knight Naberos of the Ninth Quadrant has achieved recognition due to bravery and tactical skill in battle. He has led a charge against enemy forces twice his group's number and come out the other side victorious. His title has nothing to do with his abilities, and everything to do with his skill as a leader. He is all a Knight of the Demoniac Alliance should be."

Henry hears a *click-click-click* against the back of his chair; blade-sharp nails drum against the wood, every so often grazing the collar of Henry's shirt. He can taste his heart in his throat and swallows hard to force it back down.

"Thank you, Sergeant Malephor." Nathan is doing a poor job at hiding a smile. "Please take a seat. There's enough food for everyone."

Malephor retracts her hand and takes a step forward, straightening up. "That is appreciated, sir, but not necessary. I am here to collect the human."

"*Henry*. My name is Henry."

Malephor shoots him a radioactive glare. Henry shrinks in his seat.

"Cassandra is ready to do the reading with him, as requested. Now. At this very moment," she adds in Henry's direction, as if she knows he'd rather be cooked for breakfast himself than let her take him anywhere.

However, this is Cassandra's reading for Lucy. She promised last night and is coming through. She's going to try to find out what happened to Lucy on the day she disappeared—and where she is now. There's no way Henry can pass up getting the answers he needs, even if that means he has to be shown to Cassandra by her freaky demon bodyguard.

"Well guys, that's my cue." He rises from his seat with an exaggerated sigh and claps his hands against his legs. "Wish me luck."

"Be nice to the demon" is all Tresser says as he is led out of the room.

Malephor doesn't talk as she leads him through the house. Henry is grateful for it.

He doesn't hate her by any means, but, well—Malephor is a demon. To be fair, so is Nathan, but he's not...a *demon* demon. For the most part, Nathan is a normal guy. He looks as plain and unassuming as anyone you might meet on the street. He speaks informally, he tells jokes...he acts like a human being. It's easy for Henry to forget that he isn't just a regular guy.

Malephor...now, *there's* a demon.

It wasn't just the Battle Royale last night—though, yeah, that was more than a little terrifying. Henry isn't intimidated by people just because he's aware they could crush him like a bug. It's Malephor's *attitude*. She's got the bearing of a soldier, and the ferocity of an assassin. She looks ready to take down an enemy at any moment. While that makes her an excellent bodyguard, her merits as a drinking buddy fall flat.

She'd probably attract a few stares out in public anyhow, and not in a good way. Nathan might look like a human, by Malephor is all demon. The mass of curls that flare around her head seem to glimmer, like a starry midnight; Henry could almost call it beautiful. Her pitch-black skin gleams like oil, however; intricate silver and gold designs line her toned arms and shoulders, creeping up her neck. They probably mean *something,* but Henry couldn't tell you what. The most striking thing about her, however, is her eyes—serpent's eyes, an electric green that gleam like radium, intersected by slick golden pupils.

Malephor looks every bit the creature from hell that she is. For Henry—who's barely breaking five-foot-four and is always losing his contact lenses—she's more than intimidating.

So, he doesn't *dislike* Malephor. He's just terrified of her.

There's a bit more dignity to that. At least, he hopes so.

Cassandra is ready for him once Malephor ushers him into a dimly lit back room. It smells like dried flowers and incense here. The room's wide windows are covered by heavy damask curtains, masking all light from view. Cassandra is perched on a small ottoman across from the couch, with a glass table in between them. A bowl of water sits in front of her. The array of candles ringing the table make shadows dance along the walls, filling the room with an eerie sort of warmth that swallows up Henry in an instant.

"Hey. Take a seat." She smiles at him, almost conspiratorially, as if the two of them are sharing a secret. "Let's see what we can get today."

Once again, the full reality of how *out of his depth* he is doesn't sink in until he's sitting in the middle of Cassandra's living room, watching her work. It feels like something out of a movie. Part of Henry isn't sure he hasn't fallen into one.

The psychic has the bowl of water in front of her, and she's staring down into it like it's the latest summer blockbuster. His hands are clasped in hers. A picture of Lucy -- the one he's carried around in his pocket ever since she vanished -- is between them. Casandra's eyes are half-closed. Her pupils flicker beneath hooded eyelids. It's fascinating to watch, but just as bewildering.

"I see Lucy," Cassandra announces, and that's when Henry realizes just how *crazy* this whole thing is.

Until last night, he didn't know the first thing about demons, psychics, Hell, or high water. All he knew was Lucy was missing, and he needed to find her.

(The last time he saw Lucy was a Wednesday morning, when she stumbled into the kitchen bleary-eyed, her blonde curls tangled up in a bedheaded mop, to find him dressed and ready for school.

"Morning," he greeted, and she gave a sleepy murmur of response as she slumped against the counter. Henry pressed a cup of coffee in her hands. Her viridescent eyes lit up. He watched the smile spread across her face like a flower opening to the morning sunshine.

"Last day of school," she remarked once the caffeine rendered her a little more awake. "We should celebrate."

"We've got a whole summer to ourselves," Henry agreed, stirring scrambled eggs on the stove. "We shouldn't just celebrate. We should have a party. A whole rave. What d'you think?"

Lucy's laugh rang through the kitchen like the trill of windchimes. "Save the partying for the wedding," she chided, twining her arms around Henry's neck. Smiling, he leaned back into her arms. "Only one month to go."

One month would be too long to wait. He's said this to Lucy often enough by now he knows she'll just laugh at him. Instead, he turns around, wraps his arms around her waist, and pulls her into a kiss.

They stayed twined together until the acrid smell of something burning reached his nose. Lucy pulled away with a gasp. "Henry! The eggs!"

They ate breakfast together, and then Henry had to go spend a final day at work with his second graders. He left Lucy sitting at the kitchen counter, hair falling in her face as sun streaming from the kitchen window cast her in a golden light.

He made it home that afternoon. Lucy did not.)

"What's happening?" asks Henry, leaning closer to look into the bowl of water himself. He sees nothing but morning sunlight gleaming off the surface of the liquid, and the flicker of the candle flame positioned beneath the bowl. He certainly doesn't see his fiancée in there—he can't even see his own reflection.

"She's...in a building," murmurs Cassandra, gaze fixed on the water. "Some sort of office...I don't know. She's wearing a suit. She has a necklace on."

Henry's breath catches in his throat. "A pendant? Like, like an amulet thingy? Gold, with green and blue stones?"

"That's it," says Cassandra. "She's walking down a hallway."

A hallway. Okay. That could be literally anywhere in the world. "Great. Where?"

"A building," Cassandra replies, the tone of her voice telling Henry to shut up even if her words don't. "She's— wait, something's happening."

Henry leans closer as he watches the psychic's face change. Cassandra's brows knit together. Her lips purse, eyes narrowing. Just as suddenly as the expression came over her, her mouth drops open in shock. Henry doesn't know what she's seeing, but it can't be good.

"What, what?" he demands, but Cassandra is silent for a moment that drags on for an eternity.

When she finally looks up, her eyes are still wide. There's a terseness to her jaw that makes Henry's blood run cold. Suddenly he finds himself unable to breathe. "What happened?"

Cassandra swallows hard. She seems to hesitate, as if she really doesn't want to say whatever she just saw out loud. Dread has Henry in a chokehold. He leans forward, fighting off desperation. "What?"

Cassandra breaks with a tiny sigh. Her shoulders slump. "Lucy... I watched her be taken by a demon. She was trying to get out of the building when it...grabbed her. It seemed like the same thing that came after me, its energy was the same. It just...swallowed her up. When it vanished, she was gone too."

Henry's stomach lurches. The same thing that tried to get to Cassandra ate Lucy?

"I couldn't feel much from her after the demon closed in, but...she was scared, Henry. She didn't have any way to fight back, but she was thinking of you. Her mind was going back to happier times with you the moment she was taken."

Henry tries to take a breath, but it is caught in his throat by a sob. A hand flies up to cover his mouth, and he squeezes his eyes shut in an effort to calm down. He's not going to lose it now. He can't break down now when Lucy's out there somewhere and needs him to help her.

"Where is she?" he manages once he's able to speak again. Cassandra's eyes fall to the floor.

"I don't know. I'm sorry. I couldn't see anything else after the demon took her."

His heart is in his throat as he springs to his feet. Desperation has its claw locked around his neck, and it's strangling him. "What about where she was? The office, did you get that? Where did she disappear from?"

Cassandra holds out a hand, urging Henry to sit once more. He does, but he feels so charged with adrenaline that it's impossible to hold still. "I think I found a location. Washington Avenue, on the corner of Mercer Street. It's a big white building with a fountain in front of it. Some sort of law firm."

Why would Lucy be at a law firm? That doesn't make sense. She worked in a bookshop, not as a lawyer. There's no reason she should have anything to do with an office building in general, unless she was visiting a friend. Lucy mentioned nothing about her plans for that day—Henry assumed she was going to work as normal.

That doesn't matter. He's got Lucy's last known location, and he knows the place where she vanished. It's the biggest lead he's had in weeks.

"Thanks, Cassie," he says, rising to his feet. "I'll go tell the others. It's time to get moving."

"Well, David Tresser has confined me to my house"—it's impossible to miss the scorn in Cassandra's voice—"but if I can do anything else, Henry, you've got my number. I'll help in whatever way I can."

Henry gives the psychic a thin smile. Cassandra's kind eyes quell the anxiety swirling in his stomach just enough that he finds himself able to breathe once more. "Thanks," he says again, and claps Cassandra on the shoulder. "You've been a bigger help than I can say already."

No matter why Lucy was at that office, he's going there. If he can't find her, he'll find some trace she was there. He's got to find *something*.

Henry is going to get her back, no matter what he has to do.

HE'S ABLE TO keep a steady head through the entire car ride—which is kind of a miracle, considering he's crammed in the back of a hearse. There's no dead body in here, which is a plus, he supposes. At this point, things are so weird that he's willing to take whatever tiny piece of *normal* he can get.

However, with nothing else to do, he's stuck listening to Nathan and Tresser banter like an old married couple. That's as fun as it sounds.

"I thought we were supposed to turn right."

"No, nope. Mercer Street is down here. Trust me, Nate."

"You just came to town yesterday. How do you know where you're going?"

"Well, Nate, that's because I've got a thing called intuition. Hasn't let me down before, so it's not about to start now."

"You know what really never lets you down? A map."

"Sure, if you want to be boring about it."

It's enough to drive anyone insane.

Henry isn't sure whether Tresser and Nathan get on appallingly well, or just appallingly. Their personalities contrast each other to the point that it's amazing they can stand to be in the same room. Nathan is levelheaded, stern, and sarcastic; Tresser seems to not care about anything and roll with whatever is thrown at him. Then again, Henry remembers how Tresser tore through the streets to reach Cassandra last night. He can't say Tresser doesn't care; he only *pretends* not to.

It comes down to the way they both operate. They've got the same plan here (stopping the freaking apocalypse, apparently). Their styles mesh well together, and they share the desire to get the job done. A common goal can unite anybody, Henry's learned. Spending most of the year in a room with twenty five-year-olds, teaching them to share and not to hit one another, has taught him a thing or two about people getting along. He's pretty sure Nathan and Tresser are the types of people who just click with each other. If his six years of kindergarten have taught him anything, it's that some people are just going to be friends, and when that happens, not much is capable of splitting them apart.

Still, Henry isn't sure how much more of this he can take. He never thought he'd say this, but he finds himself missing Malephor. If she weren't playing guard dog for Cassandra, she could have been able to come along; instead, he's stuck with the lovebirds, and all it's doing is reminding Henry of how depressing his own love life is.

Maybe that's a good thing. Eyes on the prize, head in the game. If he keeps thinking about Lucy, that means he'll be able to find her faster, right?

So he lets the two clowns up front figure out where they're headed and has the good sense not to help them, (even though he *lives* in this town and has a better idea of its streets than either of them).

By the time they pull up in front of Pagett and Associates Law Office, Henry is antsy for more reasons than one. He needs to be out of this car. The hearse is creepy, Nathan and Tresser are giving him a headache, and the longer he sits still, the more he feels like he's doing nothing to help Lucy. He leaps out before Tresser has put the thing in Ppark, and narrowly avoids getting backed over.

"If I kill you, it won't be my fault, you can't sue," Tresser says as he opens his own door. "What, did Cassie's ghost follow us here? Why the hell are you in such a rush?"

"*Lucy,*" is all Henry says, and all he needs to say.

"She's not going to be sitting in the lobby waiting for you." Tresser rolls his eyes. Instead of starting towards the building, however, he pauses and leans back against the car, taking it in. His eyes seem to be scanning for something—a weakness, maybe, a way they can slip in undetected. Henry doesn't know much about what Tresser does, but he has the sense that he's good at getting places he isn't supposed to be.

Nathan is staring up at the building too, albeit with a less critical expression. He's eyeing the marble fountain with disdain and seems put off by the entire structure. They must not have law firms where he comes from—that, or Nathan has a distaste for lawyers in general.

"What should we do?" Nathan asks after a moment. Tresser presses his lips together and runs a hand through his uncombed hair.

"The front door looks nice. Let's try that."

Somehow Henry just *knows* that marching right up to the front door is a bad idea; if he knows, however, that means the two professionals he's with know too. If they're walking into a hornet's nest (and the closer they get to the building, the more Henry suspects that they are), they must know what they're doing.

"All right," Nathan comments sideways, slowing his steps just enough to keep up with Henry. "The best thing you can do is stay quiet. Avoid getting hit by any flying black orbs. Don't let anyone kill you. Stay quiet, and you should be fine."

"What if I die?" Henry hisses.

Nathan doesn't flinch. "You'll figure it out."

He can feel the air growing heavier as they step into the lobby, and his stomach drops. It's exactly like it was back in that police station. There is the sense of being watched from every angle; invisible claws reach out, trying to snare you, and serpent's fangs snap at your heels. He swallows hard, forcing himself to square up as he marches alongside Nathan and Tresser.

Tresser has his hand tucked in his jacket pocket, a deceptively casual gesture. Nathan doesn't even bother. As they march up to the front desk, Nathan steps back to allow his human companion to take the lead.

"Hi," Tresser says, smiling at the secretary. "Can you help me with something?"

The secretary looks up from her computer as peers at them from over the rims of her glasses. Just for a second, her blue eyes flash black.

It feels like Henry's been impaled by an icicle. There is a genuine *demon* in this woman, he realizes. His eyes widen, and it's all he can do not to go sprinting back out the door.

Tresser and Nathan stand their ground, though, so he does too—even if he feels two seconds away from passing out.

After a beat, the secretary smiles. "That's what I'm here for!" she replies in a cloyingly cheerful voice, leaning towards them. "How can I help you, sir?"

"We're looking for a missing girl, so we need to see any security tapes you've got on hand from the past few weeks. Mind letting us have a look?"

The woman purses her lips. "Hmm, sorry, sir. I can't do that."

Tresser leans forward, both hands on the desk in front of him. "Sorry to hear that. Thing is, we need those tapes, and we're going to get them. *You* don't have much choice."

"I disagree." The secretary sits up straight, pleasant smile still on her face. "In fact, I have to ask you to leave now."

For a moment, no one flinches. Nathan remains still as a statue at Tresser's side, entire body tensed; he is the perfect guard dog, ready to snap. Tresser is oozing charm like a cobra seconds before striking, eyes sharp as daggers. Henry can feel his heart pounding against his ribcage. The tension feels like it's strangling him, but he forces himself not to breathe too loudly. All he can do is watch and wait.

He's gotten very good at waiting.

(He waited at the restaurant for half an hour before he started getting really worried.

It wasn't like Lucy to be late. She prided herself on punctuality. Even if she could be disorganized with little things, like leaving her clothes lying around or forgetting to clean up after she cooked, she made a point of never being late. "It shows people you respect them," she explained. "I like making a good impression."

By the time forty minutes slipped by, Henry already called Lucy's phone twice and left four text messages. She didn't answer his texts, which wasn't unusual, but by the third time his calls went unanswered he could feel icy water pooling in the pit of his stomach.

Lucy had him as her emergency contact. If anything happened, he would have gotten a call. He comforted himself with that as he anxiously gnawed on breadsticks, watching the restaurant door like a hawk. Any minute, she would walk through the doors. She would be harried, apologizing profusely for being late, but she would be safe and all right and there.

Any minute.)

A shrill scream of static rips through the entire building, and the glass doors explode.

Henry drops to the ground, both hands clamped over his ears. This is for the best, because a chair flies over him a second later; just a little slower, and his head would have been taken clean off. It hits the wall behind the desk instead, exploding into wooden shards. The secretary doesn't even flinch. Her eyes are pitch black as she springs from her seat, and with one leap, she stands on top of the counter, reaching for Tresser's throat.

Tresser is too fast for her. He whips a knife from his pocket and slices it across her outstretched arm. Flesh sizzles; Henry is assaulted with the smell of burning chicken grease as the demon reels back. Smoke is seeping from the deep gash on her arm.

She isn't alone, though, and they're outnumbered. At least fifteen office workers spring to the attack. In seconds the group finds themselves walled in on all sides. The demons are all but frothing from the mouth; their eyes are a numbing, empty pitch black that seems to suck all the light from around them. As one swipes at him with black-clawed hands, Henry lets out a yell and cringes back.

"We probably could have planned this better," Tresser announces.

Nathan glances over his shoulder. "I thought you liked to improvise?"

Tresser considers this for a moment. "Screw it, you're right," he declares, before jabbing his knife at the nearest demonic head.

The chaos after that is too much for Henry to keep up with; he sure doesn't try. He hasn't had the military training of Nathan or the guidance of whoever the hell taught Tresser to shoot like that. He can't fight monsters. All he can do is keep his head down and hope he doesn't get killed.

It's a near miss once, when a demonic office worker notices him crouched behind a potted plant and leaps at him, mouth filled with razor-sharp fangs. Nathan leaps in between them at the last moment. He slams his fist into the side of the demon's head, taking it down, and kicks it again to make sure it stays there. He doesn't spare Henry a backwards glance.

Henry watches the two of them fight in tandem with a sort of awe he usually reserved for really cool action movies. They might have nothing on giant robots battling it out in the middle of New York, but Tresser and Nathan are their own sort of special effects. When one moves, the other follows. Where Nathan swings, Tresser is just as quick to aim. No matter how many demons come at them at once, they have each other's back. It is a breathtaking, choreographed, lethal dance.

They slip up just once, and it's when Tresser is dueling the secretary. She's got burning gashes across her face and arms, which spew black smoke around her. It is easy to see how she is more monster than human, but if Tresser is perturbed, he doesn't show it. He's locked in ironclad concentration: to take the demon out without killing the host.

Just as he lands a well-placed blow to the demon's gut, sending her doubling over, a roar sounds from behind him. He looks back for a split second—all the time he needs to see the burly, black-eyed security guard fling himself on Nathan.

Henry has just enough time to realize the demon has a knife of his own before it's coming down towards Nathan's head. Caught in his own battle, Nathan doesn't see, doesn't notice.

Tresser does.

He slams into the demon like a train hitting a truck. They both go flying; the knife hits the ground and skitters out of reach. Henry is close enough to snatch it up without being noticed and hugs it close to him as he watches Tresser and the demon struggle on the ground.

The demon outweighs Tresser by a good hundred pounds, but Tresser is feral. He claws at the guy's beard, swings with knees and elbows—and at the first opportunity, knees the man between the legs.

Henry winces. He'd better not pick any fights with Tresser.

The demon roars in pain. That's all the opportunity Tresser needs to turn the tables on him. He slams the butt of his gun into the man's head once, twice, three times, until he has gone still.

By the time he shoves the demon off of him, Nathan is just incapacitating the secretary who started it all. One quick jab to the neck sends her crumpling, and Nathan is left standing over at least twenty unmoving bodies.

He offers a hand to Tresser. The other man takes it, shoulders heaving, breath coming in harsh pants. Together, they stand over the carnage, hands clasped between them.

"You saved my life," says Nathan. He looks surprised, and more than a little impressed.

Tresser just shrugs. "Pretend you owe me one now."

Very slowly, Henry rises from the safety of his potted plant.

"Holy hell," he moans. "Are you guys machines? Are you actually Terminators? Who trained you? Where did you come from?"

"Hell," Nathan answers frankly.

"Washington," Tresser says with a grin.

When Henry hands the knife over (because he sure doesn't want it), Nathan frowns down at the engraved handle.

"This athame was made by hand. Someone knew what they were doing."

"Not a friend?" Henry guesses.

Nathan flips the knife in his hands. "Let's just say there are very few ways to kill a High Demon. Overwhelming it à la Malephor is one method. Stabbing one with a blade made by another high demon, specifically to kill their brethren, is another."

"Nate, I'm just gonna guess someone knows you're here," Tresser murmurs, "and they're not happy about it."

Nathan frowns down at the knife for a second longer before shaking his head and slipping it into his belt. "A bit of opposition only means we're on the right track," he says. His words spark a fire in Henry's chest; it's only intensified when Nathan looks up at him. "Now where did Cassandra say she last saw Lucy?"

THE STAIRCASE DOOR swings open, and a weight Henry didn't realize he was carrying lifts from his chest. Every beat of his heart pounds against his ribcage; he is ready to charge forward before a hand catches him by the shoulder. He spins around, an exclamation of annoyance already on his lips, but it dies when he sees the expression on Nathan's face.

"Something was here," the demon says, gazing into the fluorescent-lit hallway. It is as if he can see something Henry cannot. "Not anymore, but something was here. Something powerful."

Henry's skin prickles. He feels nauseous with anticipation; the sheer knowledge that Lucy was here when she was taken is almost too much to bear. He stares down the hallway, searching for any sign of her, but somehow, he can't take the first step. He can't push himself to go in with the *something powerful* hanging over his head.

The three linger in the doorway for a moment, hardly daring to breathe. Finally, Tresser lets out a loud sigh and is the first to step into the stairwell. "Nate, this is a law firm. If this place doesn't unsettle you, then people aren't doing their jobs."

Henry's mind flashes back to the throng of people they just exorcized in the lobby. "*That* goes without saying."

He follows in Tresser's footsteps, feeling a flash of guilt for not being first through the door. He can't help the way his limbs drag. Something about seeing this hallway, knowing it's where Lucy was taken, chills him to the bone. These walls were the last thing she saw. He pictures her, with her bouncing curls and high-heeled shoes, reaching out towards the door, desperate to get there before whatever was after her could steal her away—

She didn't make it. She vanished, alone in a cold, concrete-floored hallway. She didn't have a chance.

Baby, what were you doing here?

"Henry!" Nathan's sudden voice jolts him out of his reverie. "You need to see this."

He spins around, eyes wide. Somehow he already knows what the object at Nathan's feet is, even before he gets close enough to see the glint of green and blue stones set in gold. The chain is broken and crumpled in a heap on the ground, but there is no mistaking Lucy's amulet.

(She wore that necklace every day. Her father gave it to her for her high school graduation.)

He leans down, closes his fist around the chain, and lifts it into the air. The amulet swings in his grasp, back and forth, back and forth. It is hypnotizing. Henry's mind flashes to the thousands of times he's seen it on Lucy's neck, and his lungs feel as if they've been filled with dry ice. Lucy hardly ever takes this off, and she'd certainly never leave it in a strange building. It's her most precious possession.

She wouldn't have left it unless she had no choice.

(He waited until an hour and a half had passed, and by then he knew something was terribly wrong.

He paid the bill for what little he'd ordered and rushed out of the restaurant. Even as he jogged, his hands were busy dialing his fiancée's coworker.

"Have you seen Lucy? Did you hear from her today?"

She never showed up at work.

He tried her best friend next. "Did Lucy call you today? Did she tell you she was going anywhere or doing anything?"

She hadn't been heard from since that morning.

Finally, he called Lucy's mother. "I can't find Lucy. She's not answering her phone. Have you heard from her at all?"

She hadn't contacted her family.

When Henry returned to their apartment, he already knew what he would find. That didn't make the sight of an empty, silent flat any less paralyzing.)

Henry tastes something bitter in his mouth. *She never had a chance,* he thinks again, and the rage boils up all at once, hot as a grease fire and twice as untamable.

"God dammit," he hisses, first clenching tight around the amulet. Then he aims a sudden kick at the wall. "God *damn it!*"

His foot bounces off painted brick, sending a shock wave of pain all the way up to his ankle. He curses again and grips the necklace to his chest, unwilling to let it go no matter what. He isn't going to lose what small part of Lucy he still has. He doesn't realize he's screaming until the sound of his own voice reaches his ears.

"Who the hell do they think they are, taking her? What the hell are they doing to her? How could she have just disappeared? Where *is* she? Where the *fuck* is she?"

He rages and roars and doesn't come back to himself even when he sees his companions staring at him. Neither of them move; they don't know how to react and know better than to try comforting him.

There is something to be said about being the only one in the room yelling, though. In the face of Nathan and Tresser's calm, it's no longer possible to ignore his own loss of control. His breathing slowly regulates itself once more; a semblance of rational thought returns to him. As much as he burns, he knows he can't lose it now.

"I need—" he says and pauses to inhale a ragged breath. "I have to save her."

"I know, Henry," says Nathan, low and solemn. There is no judgment in his voice. "We're going to find her."

"No," Henry says, because he doesn't get it, and he needs them both to understand. "*I'm* getting her back. I am going to get her back, no matter what I have to do. I'm going to find her and bring her home."

They are both silent in the face of Henry's resolution. They understand what Henry is saying; his words couldn't be clearer. If he has to take on an entire demon army himself, he will. If he has to walk through fire, he will. He's going to bring Lucy home.

Tresser takes a step forward then. He doesn't reach out, but there is an understanding in his eyes that can't be ignored. "Yes," he says, nodding slowly. "You will."

"I will." Henry feels the rage drain out of him all at once, replaced by grief and exhaustion. He is so *exhausted*—he's been doing this for a month, and he's tired.

He can't rest until he finds her. Looking down at the necklace in his hand, it dawns on him that this is his first concrete lead. It's the biggest clue he's gotten, the best, and if there's any way it can be used to find where Lucy is now—

"I need you guys with me on this," he says, meeting the eyes of both men in turn. "Say you'll help me."

Nathan offers a solemn nod. Tresser mirrors his action, saluting Henry with two fingers.

"Nate. David," Henry says, and feels the names burn as they dance off his tongue. "I guess this means we have each other's backs."

It might take everything he's got, but he meant what he said. He's bringing Lucy home if it's the last thing he does.

Chapter Five

CASSANDRA DOESN'T GET many houseguests.

That goes without saying. She lives alone, out in the middle of nowhere, in a town so white collar and ordinary on its surface that she's amazed she wasn't burned as a witch the moment she stepped onto Main Street. Cassandra lives out in the woods because she knew there was no place for her in town. For the most part, she's comfortable with the solitude.

It's not like she's alone. She might not have any family left, but she's got friends. There's Adam down at the bookshop, always helpful whenever she needs new spell ingredients or books. There are a few psychics on the local college campus who sometimes meet up with her. She knows how helpful guidance from someone with a bit more experience can be when you're figuring out your abilities, so she tries to be as helpful, and available, as possible. She was close with Sophie, before...well, before.

Plus, there's always the *others*. The others are everywhere. They appear to her in visions, dreams, across from her in the coffee shop or whispering in her ear in the dead of night. There is no escaping them. They are as constant as the moon itself, and numerous as the stars.

When the dead won't leave you alone, there's very little need for human company.

Cassandra's gotten used to being alone. She enjoys it. That's not an exaggeration, nothing she's trying to convince herself of to feel less pitiful. It's true. She's spent most of her time alone from a young age, and it's peaceful. Loneliness has never sunk its claws into her.

So, she isn't sure what to do with her newly appointed bodyguard.

Malephor's a demon, sure, but that isn't the weird thing. Cassandra has met demons before. They're a species, as much as human or spirit or any other entity. Calling all of them bad—the kind of demons who possess people to hurt them—is a gross generalization. There are as many good demons as there are good people, so Malephor being a demon isn't the strange part.

It's more…Malephor being here at all, really.

"Sooo," Cassandra says, once they're left alone in the house. "What do you like to do for fun?"

"Nothing," Malephor answers promptly.

"Nothing?"

"I am a Sergeant, a courier, and a soldier of the Demoniac Alliance. I do not do anything for 'fun'."

"Oh," says Cassandra. "That's neat. How…how about knitting? You look like a knitter."

Malephor doesn't know how to knit. This becomes obvious when she shreds the yarn with her claws (she's supposed to look human, *why* does she have claws?) within the first five minutes. The television bothers her enough that she snarls at it. She can't understand the rules of Connect Four and melted one of the Monopoly pieces. Cassandra is too afraid to try Jenga.

Finally, out of desperation, she settles on the simplest game she can think of.

"Tic…tac…toe." She draws a line across the tiny page of notebook paper and looks up at Malephor in satisfaction. "I win again!"

Malephor's bright green eyes are locked on her, wide and focused. It would be a little uncomfortable, but Cassandra is used to it. Most dead people are kind of...*intense*. She can handle intense.

"I don't like this game," Malephor tells her. "I preferred the Hanging Man."

Two rounds into hangman, Cassandra decided the demon was getting too excited. They're not going back to hangman. "Why? This is fun, isn't it?"

She blinks at Malephor for a few seconds, smile determinedly set on her face. For a long moment, Malephor glowers, making her opinion on the game clear; then, to Cassandra's surprise, the demon relaxes. As much as a demon can relax, anyway. "It's not bad," she answers. "Okay."

Okay. Well, it's something. Cassandra will take it.

Slowly, Malephor straightens up, and Cassandra summons the reserves of her energy to do the same. She didn't sleep well last night; with visions of demons dancing through her head, that's no surprise. She also knows for a fact that Malephor didn't sleep either. She could see her silhouette from the hallway, sitting up through the night. Malephor stayed wide awake, guarding her. Waiting for an attack that may not come.

That same intensity is present in her gaze now. Cassandra straightens up under it. It feels like her every move is being noticed.

She pushes herself away from the table, allowing her gaze to rest on Malephor for a single second, before conjuring up a smile. "Well, sounds like coffee will be needed," she says. "You want some?"

"Coffee?" Malephor echoes, sounding thoughtful. "Never had it."

"That settles it, then." Cassandra flashes the demon a wink. "I'll be back."

She's already turned towards the kitchen when Malephor's voice pipes up. "If anything happens—"

She cuts herself off when Cassandra turns to look at her, eyebrows raised. Maybe she's realized how overprotective she sounds; maybe she's decided that Cassandra gets the message. Either way, Malephor's mouth shuts with a *click,* and she doesn't finish the sentence.

Cassandra waits until she's reached the relative solitude of the kitchen before she lets herself sigh. She's not sure how to feel about Malephor.

It isn't that she dislikes her. In fact, she thinks she would like Malephor very much, under the right circumstances. She seems like an interesting person. When she speaks, her words are laced with flashes of quicksilver cleverness that catch Cassandra's attention instantly. Her eyes are a sharp electric green, skin an inky black, lined with the occasional flashes of what Cassandra is sure are scales. She holds herself like she's ready for anything and has proved that to be the case. Malephor, as Cassandra realized the second she defeated the demon outside her house, is fearless.

Her gifts allow her a certain empathy. She has always been skilled at understanding people, but being able to feel an echo of what they feel certainly helps. Usually, Cassandra has no trouble reading people. Trying to understand Malephor, though, feels like puzzling over a book written in another language. Cassandra doesn't know where to start, but she wants to figure out what it says.

It takes a bit of thought to identify her feelings as awe. She respects the demon, but she does not fear her... though Malephor has made it clear that her abilities are to be feared). In spite of her better judgement, Cassandra is fascinated by her.

What she *doesn't* like is being under house arrest, stuck under the care of a demon bodyguard who feels more like a babysitter.

It's not Malephor's fault. She's performing her duties admirably. Cassandra, however, doesn't need to be protected. No one has to take care of her. She's perfectly capable of doing that herself. Suddenly losing her own agency and having her wellbeing entrusted to a demon is...unsettling.

People don't look after her. That's the way it's always been. She takes care of herself. The sudden implication she can't, isn't just demeaning, it's *infuriating*.

Geez, could you be any tougher on that machine? Watch out, the coffee might decide to spit back.

Cassandra blinks down at her hands and realizes she's been taking out her frustration on her coffee maker. The very *expensive* coffee maker that her mother bought her as a housewarming gift many years ago. She's in no hurry to break this machine, especially since half of her blood is basically coffee by this point. If she went into caffeine withdrawal, she's pretty sure she'd die.

"Sorry," she mutters, closing the coffee maker gently and pressing the button to allow it to brew. A huff sounds, close enough she can feel a chill against the side of her neck.

What's got you all twist-and-snappy? George asks, leaning forward from his perch on the kitchen counter. *Don't tell me you're letting Malicious get under your skin that much.*

"I'm not," Cassandra says immediately. "And don't use nicknames. They don't work for you. Get off the counter."

George rolls his eyes, but obligingly hops down. His feet make no sound when they connect with the tiled floor, and no shadow is cast as he stands in the faint kitchen light. This isn't a surprise. Ghosts don't tend to leave much of a physical presence.

George likes sitting on furniture. He's like an overgrown, snarky cat, and Cassandra hasn't decided whether she should just deal with it or try to ghost-proof her house. The night she found George swinging on the chandelier, she almost had a heart attack, and the ghost takes particular delight in sitting on top of Cassandra's television while she's watching it.

That's just the type of person George Soto is—unpredictable, adventurous, and a little bit exhausting. He's one of the best friends Cassandra's had in years.

Maybe that's sad. She figures it is... but at this point, after so many years of self-imposed isolation from society, she'll take what she can get. She's been helping spirits since childhood, but most don't bother sticking around to get to know her. George is different.

She's not sure exactly when George got attached to her, but for the past month, the ghost has been following her around as if Cassandra is his new best friend. In many ways, that's true.

Cassandra is the only one that can see him, and George has a way of drawing energy that makes him impossible to ignore. Cassandra doubts she could block George out if she wanted to, and most of the time she doesn't. It's nice to have someone around. Even if George talks too much, teases her, and tells awful jokes, he's still company. As Cassandra is aware, that's something that's been in short supply recently.

(She doesn't mind the isolation, really. She's never lonely...but sometimes she can't help feeling *alone.*)

Now, though, George has his chin balanced in his hand, looking like the cat that caught the canary. This is how Cassandra knows he must be bored. A bored George latches onto any bit of gossip he can find. When he's bingeing *The Real Housewives* on Cassandra's television, this is tolerable. When it's Cassandra's life...not so much.

C'mon, the chick's terrifying. You're telling me the whole 'silent but spooky' thing doesn't get under your skin?

It really doesn't. That's just how Malephor is. It doesn't seem threatening to Cassandra, and she's certainly not going to begrudge her for her natural personality. It's not even a *bad* personality. "No, it doesn't. It...it suits her."

Oh? George sounds intrigued. Then, after a few seconds, he snickers. *Ohhh.*

"What *oh?*" Cassandra gets the feeling she doesn't want to know, but this won't stop George either way.

You like her. That's why you're being so damn hospitable. You think Miss Mal is hot.

Cassandra chokes on air, and winds up sputtering for a minute as she tries to get her breath back. She pounds on her chest, passing it off as a coughing fit to keep George from jeering. It's useless. When she turns back, she finds the ghost watching with rapt attention, eyes just barely hidden behind shaggy bangs, smirk fixed on his lips.

"Are you crazy? I don't like her. I just met her," Cassandra says, and hopes she doesn't sound defensive.

You still think she's hot, George replies matter-of-factly. *Not like I'm blaming you. I mean, hey, those eyes could stop a train in its tracks, am-i-rite? And the scales?* Wow.

"I'm not engaging you," Cassandra replies, turning back to her coffee.

Like, if she could see me, and, you know, wasn't a she? *I'd be all over that.*

"George."

Hey, dead already, right? Not like I've got anything to be afraid of.

"George."

Sometimes you've just gotta court danger. Or sleep with it.

"George," Cassandra enunciates, and the warning in her voice is clear. George breaks into a roguish grin.

Hey, Cassie, don't worry. I support whatever choices you make. He reaches out to pat Cassandra on the shoulder, and Cassandra feels the slight chill that comes with a ghost touching her skin. She's experienced enough to keep from cringing. *Just make sure to stay safe. No biting unless it's consensual.*

"That's enough." Cassandra rolls her eyes, and fights against the smirk itching at her lips. She knows George is just being ridiculous, so there's no reason the idea of finding Malephor attractive should embarrass her at all. So what if she does...sort of agree with George's assessment? Malephor is an attractive woman. (*Demon,* she reminds herself, very *not-human.*) That's good for her. Great.

More than that, however, she's an interesting person. Cassandra might still have no clue what to do with her demonic escort, but she knows that she wants to take advantage of the time they have together. For however long Malephor is here, she's eager to get to know her.

She tells herself it's because Malephor killed the demon for her. She owes her the gratitude of learning about her—that's all.

"You could be helpful," Cassandra says as she pours the coffee into twin mugs, "and get me some sugar." She's halfway through pouring Malephor's cup before her hand goes still. "Do you think she likes sugar?"

Eh. She seems like a 'drink it black' kinda person to me. Then again, she's never had coffee before. She's got no clue what she likes. You can't go wrong!

Cassandra accepts this for the fact that it is, so she adds sugar and a splash of cream to both mugs before carrying them out to where Malephor is still waiting. (She'd never inflict black coffee on a first-timer.)

She looks almost demure—sitting at the table with her arms folded on its top, allowing serpentine eyes to wander around Cassandra's living room. She takes in the curtains, the light fixtures, the sofas, and seems particularly fixated on a few hanging pictures of Cassandra's family. There's one of her father, posing next to his shiny new convertible the day he got it. Another is of her mother in an oversized sunhat and glasses, lounging on the beach. Malephor seems most interested in a picture that Cassandra can't even remember being taken—that of her mother, father, and herself, all posing for a studio photograph. Cassandra couldn't have been more than four years old. Her corn-silk hair is pulled into pigtails, and she wears a gummy smile. Above her head, her parents beam with pride.

She catches the flicker of a smile on Malephor's lips and gets the inexplicable feeling that she's intruding on something personal. Which is ridiculous—these are *her* photos. When she clears her throat, the demon snaps to attention.

"I tried to sweeten it," Cassandra says, setting the two mugs down on the table. "If it's too strong for you, don't feel like you have to drink it. Coffee isn't for everyone."

Malephor takes the drink with a murmur of thanks and raises it to her lips. Cassandra raises an unimpressed eyebrow as her guest's face twists in disgust. For a moment she's sure Malephor is about to spew hot liquid all over the table, but she manages to choke it back. Cassandra can't help chuckling when the demon looks at her again. "Too much, right?"

"No," says Malephor. "It's great."

She doesn't get why Malephor does that—lie to save her feelings. She doesn't seem as though she has any reason to care about those things, but it's clear she does anyway. At least, around Cassandra.

Taking a sip of her own coffee, Cassandra studies Malephor over the mug's rim. "You'll be glad to know that my friend George finds you attractive."

Malephor raises an eyebrow. "Umm. Huh. Should I be flattered?"

"Depends how you feel about ghosts."

It's strange to bring up her gift so casually, but Malephor doesn't bat an eye. She smirks instead, turning from Cassandra to her coffee. In a matter of seconds, her gaze is drawn back to the photographs. She can tell Malephor wants to ask but doesn't want to offend. Cassandra saves her the trouble.

"My father died when I was eight. Car accident." She sees the way Malephor's face falls, expression closing off. It's the same reaction she gets from anyone when they learn how her father passed away—but instead of the automatic sympathy Cassandra is so used to receiving, Malephor's eyes just study her raptly. Their sharpness takes her aback.

"That was when I started seeing things," she explains. "My father was the first spirit I ever spoke to. It's all been uphill from there, I guess."

"You've been doing this for a long time," Malephor says. Her expression is still unreadable.

Seventeen years to the day that her abilities manifested. Seventeen years since Cassandra has had a night's sleep without spirits invading her dreams. Seventeen years of seeing things no one else can, of being able to feel what shouldn't be felt. Seventeen years of learning all she could, practicing as much as possible, forcing herself to understand energy, warding, and all the ways to protect herself from the day-to-day dangers of her abilities.

Cassandra doesn't resent it. It's a part of her. She's not sure who she'd be without her powers. As exhausting as it can be, she wouldn't trade being a psychic for anything.

It gives her the chance to help people. Cassandra Carlyle has been helping people since a very young age, and if her gifts allow her to do that (even for people who are no longer alive), she can do nothing but embrace them.

She looks at Malephor and is surprised by the respect in her eyes. She doesn't tell most people about her abilities; most are skeptical, or at least baffled by them.

Respect isn't something she often gets from people she's never helped, but seeing it from a virtual stranger—from Malephor—startles her.

"You've got a very powerful aura," she says at once. It's a diversion, an attempt to distract herself, and she realizes it as well as Malephor must. That doesn't stop her from talking. "It's a deep red, like wine—do you know what wine is?" The demon shakes her head. Cassandra will have to show her that, as well. "It's striking. You have a very strong personality, Mal."

Malephor shrugs. Cassandra wonders if she's imagining the hint of embarrassment on her face. "I guess," she replies, and takes another sip of coffee. When her face contorts, Cassandra can't help laughing. "You actually drink this stuff?"

"Drink it? I live off it."

Malephor's concern is plain, and she seems ready to say something stern, (to scold her like a parent—Cassandra wants to laugh again) when she suddenly goes tense. Her eyes flicker towards the grandfather clock hanging above the wall. Though she remains still, Cassandra knows what the reaction means. Less than ten seconds later, the clock's deep chime rings throughout the house.

"Just a clock," Cassandra soothes, placing a quick hand over Malephor's own. She doesn't think of it until the demon looks startled, drawing her hand back automatically. Feeling stupid, Cassandra wraps both hands around her cup.

"Clocks, coffee, and ghosts," Malephor mutters. "You sure do live an exciting life."

"Making your job worthwhile." Cassandra smirks; after a few seconds, Malephor's lips twitch in return.

They drink the rest of their coffee in silence, neither of them saying a word. It is almost comfortable, but there is a scrutiny in it that leaves Cassandra feeling as if she's being evaluated. Malephor isn't glaring anymore or even looking at her. Still, Cassandra listens to the rhythm of their breathing in the silence and knows she's being studied as much as she's studying the woman in front of her.

There is a peculiarity to silence that's neither comfortable nor unsettling. There is no urge to escape it; you do not feel the need to hide, to shield yourself from the absence of words. You feel as if you could lose yourself in it—not happily, but in a still sort of peace, not unlike death.

Cassandra thinks a lot about death. She wonders what it feels like when it comes. She wonders what follows after. Is it like a curtain falling on an empty stage, or the lights flickering out all at once to surround you in empty blackness? Does it come gradually, or do you blink out so quickly you don't even realize it? Is a part of you left behind? Does something of a person still exist, even after their spirit is gone?

For as thin as her own veil is, death still seems like a far-removed, distant thing. She cannot understand it. All efforts to learn from those who've already endured it has left her only more confused.

She has asked, over and over, what death is like—and no one has been able to give her an answer. Every spirit she has ever met has a different opinion. For some, it is painful, some it is easy, some fast and some slow, some confused and some accepting. Death is as varied as life itself. Everyone Cassandra has asked has only been able to agree on one thing.

Death is silent.

Cassandra has never really liked silence.

She drains the last of her coffee and sets it down on the table with a clink before rising to her feet. "All right."

Malephor blinks at her. Cassandra forces a smile, much more daring than she actually feels. She is tired of being confused and uncertain in her own home; she's tired of being an awful hostess. Maybe she doesn't have many visitors, but that's no excuse.

"Come on," she says to Malephor as she crosses the room. "Let's go."

"Go?" Malephor looks baffled. She also looks ready to fight, which is probably what she thinks 'go' means, but Malephor always looks like that, so Cassandra isn't alarmed.

Cassandra presses a few buttons on her old-fashioned stereo set, and it blares to life. A classic 80s pop song blares out of the speakers by a band Cassandra doesn't care to remember the name of. It's loud, bubbly, and *fun*. She grins, bouncing back over to Malephor's side.

"Come on!" she says again, holding out her hands. "Let's dance!"

Malephor is tentative. Her steps are clumsy and uncertain, not quite sure what she's doing. She's never danced with a human before, and it's obvious. Cassandra bounces up and down on her heels, swinging the demon's hands with her, and watches as Malephor's stiff posture begins to loosen up.

"Just let go," she encourages, "and dance!"

Malephor jumps. It's sudden enough that Cassandra almost falls over, but once she realizes what's happening, she grins. Malephor mirrors the expression; her sharp teeth don't look half as threatening when paired with the genuine happiness on her face. *Happy* is a wonderful look for Malephor.

Hand in hand, the two of them bounce and twirl with each other, reveling in the glorious absence of silence.

Chapter Six

THE NEXT PLACE they go is somewhat of a gamble. Henry doesn't like the idea from the start, because it feels counterproductive—they've just gotten their biggest lead, so shouldn't they keep moving forward? They could give the necklace to Cassandra and see what she comes up with. Why try something new now?

"Cassie can't see everything all the time," Tresser explains. "If she did, I could never look her in the eye. Besides, if Lucy's gone where we think, scrying wouldn't tell us anything. She can't look into Hell."

"So, then what's our next move?"

"The guy I'm going to visit now is supposed to be an expert in all things spooky. I wouldn't be surprised if he had some ideas."

For Henry, that's not good enough—but Nathan seems like he's on board with the plan, so it's two against one. Still, Henry feels the burn of the amulet in the pocket of his shirt, and it fuels his reluctance. "But if Cassie could—"

"If this guy can't help, then we'll go to Cassie. If Cassie can't help... well, then we're out of luck."

"Don't say that," Nathan admonishes before turning back to Henry. "Hell has its own army. We're not the only ones focused on finding the missing people, and they'll probably have an easier time of it than we will. We're not nearly out of options—we're just getting started. Let's try this first."

Henry has to agree—but that doesn't mean he's happy about it.

By the time they pull up in front of *Lehexe's Books*, it's well past noon and the shop-filled avenue is coming to life. It's hard to find a parking spot for the conspicuous hearse. When Henry climbs out the back, he feels sure the throngs of potential customers are gaping at them.

Used to the attention, or otherwise not caring, Tresser breezes past a gaggle of window-shopping soccer moms and pushes open the bookstore doors. Nathan and Henry trail after him, one curious and one reluctant.

The shop isn't half as crowded as the street outside, which is a relief. It is a quaint, nook-in-the-wall place, with walls lined with shelves from floor to ceiling. It reminds Henry of the place Lucy used to work—it is comfortable and feels *safe*. A few people browse the shelves, while an old man is purchasing a stack of books. The counter is manned by a petite girl with dark skin and large, birdlike eyes. They flicker up to the newcomers as they enter the shop, but almost immediately return to the customer at hand. The man bids her a good day, and she responds with a smile that looks tight on her thin face— almost as if she's forgotten how to smile, and she has to remind herself to do so.

Tresser doesn't hesitate to step up to the counter. "Is Adam Lehexe here?"

The girl blinks at him, and Henry catches a flash of something suspicious in her eyes. It's not fear, not quite, but it's darker than curiosity. "He is," she replies after a moment. "He's in the back."

"Can you go get him, please? I need to speak with him, now."

The girl hesitates. Tresser crosses his arms to show that he'll wait, and she takes two steps back towards a door behind the counter without looking away from them. Henry isn't sure what's making the situation more tense—Tresser's straightforward approach or the girl's timidness.

She opens the door and calls back a name, but the person who comes through the door isn't what Henry expected. He doesn't look like a bookshop owner at all. He's tall and freckled, with bright ginger hair and large eyes that take in the "customers" with less suspicion than the girl. He looks almost friendly; until he takes in the confusion in his coworker's face, and the stony expression on Tresser's.

"Can I help you?" he asks, stepping up with a smile that seems forced. Tresser's frown deepens.

"Unless you're Adam Lehexe, no. You're not Adam Lehexe. Can I speak to him, or am I gonna have to meet-and-greet the whole staff first?"

The kid's pleasant smile remains fixed in place. He's got experience in customer service. "Mr. Lehexe is unable to come to the desk right now, but I'd be glad to help you in the meantime."

Tresser pauses, shoots the kid a displeased look, and then sighs heavily. "Tell him," he says, "that Mr. Tresser of the Tresser Corporation is here to speak with him. He'll find a way to get down here."

Whatever effect Tresser was expecting his words to have, the kid's reaction probably isn't it. His eyes widen, and he draws back from the counter like he's been slapped. His mouth drops open in mute astonishment. He gapes for a minute before managing to come out with, "Oh man! You guys are part of that shifty corporation thing!"

Nathan raises an eyebrow, while Tresser just sighs again. Henry tries not to show how baffled he feels and fails miserably. "You're the ones looking for the not-dead people!" the kid exclaims—and then stops, mouth shutting with a click.

He knows he's said too much right away, and it's only confirmed when Tresser stands up straighter. Suddenly the tension in the room has taken a level up. Looking around, Henry realizes the rest of the store has cleared out. It's just him, Nathan, and Tresser, against these two clerks who apparently aren't as hapless as they seem.

"Beck, really?" the girl hisses.

Beck's eyes are still wide. "I shouldn't have mentioned that," he declares. "That was a thing I shouldn't have said."

Tresser's entire body is tense. His shoulders are a rigid line; his jaw could slice glass to shards. He leans in, causing Beck to back into his other coworker, and narrows his eyes at them as if deciphering some sort of code.

Finally, he speaks. "You two are going to have to come with me."

The girl's reaction is immediate. She jumps, hands locking around her taller coworker's shoulders and digging in like claws. Beck doesn't wince. He stands up taller, defiant, and has the guts to shake his head. "We can't do that, buddy," he replies. "We just work here."

"You might work here, but you shouldn't *be* here," Tresser retorts. "You're both supposed to be dead, aren't you?"

Beck's jaw is tight with tension; the girl behind him looks scared half to death. "That isn't true."

"It is. You can't lie to me, kid."

"I'm not lying," Beck retorts, but the small quaver in his voice gives him away. He takes a step back, and Henry doesn't blame him. Tresser is intense in a way none of them have ever seen before, locked on to these retail workers like a starving dog after a steak bone. It's both frightening and confusing. Nathan's face betrays little emotion, but Henry can tell the demon is as baffled as he is.

"You're coming with us," Tresser says again. The boy quickly shakes his head.

"No, we're not. We were just—we're just—"

The door opens so suddenly it startles them all. Henry jumps half a foot into the air and grips Nathan's shoulder. The girl behind the counter looks one strong gust of wind away from passing out.

"Is something going on here?"

When the man steps through the doorway, Henry's first thought is that he doesn't look like a bookshop owner either. Tall, slender, with dark skin and darker eyes, the man does not look like he belongs behind the counter of a retail store. He calls to mind the image of some avenging angel, the type Henry used to see in murals when dragged to church as a kid. He looks stern, yet also just, and has a quiet presence that commands attention instantly. Somehow Henry knows that this is the notorious Adam Lehexe.

Tresser must recognize him too, because he takes a step forward. "Mr. Lehexe," he says, nodding his head. "I'm David Tresser, and I've got some questions for you. A lot, actually. First, I'm going to have to take these two into custody."

"Custody?" Lehexe spits the word, looking incredulous. "Why?"

"Because you're harboring two very dangerous individuals who less than a few weeks ago were six feet under. Am I right?" One look at Lehexe's face, and those of his workers', confirms it. "I'm right. The Tresser Corporation is dealing with these cases, so I'll need to take them in."

Lehexe crosses his arms, and breezes past the kids to step up to the counter. "That's not happening," he replies levelly. "These kids are under my protection."

Something in Tresser's expression twitches. "I wasn't asking. It's sweet that you want to protect them, but you don't know what these people are doing."

"Yes, I do. Knowing things is my job."

"It's mine, too. Thing is, I also have to deal with them." Tresser refocuses on the two kids, who shrink back as if he's made a grab for them. For one awful second, Henry is sure Tresser is going to do just that—then Lehexe steps in again, eyes blazing with something that sends an icy jolt down Henry's spine.

"If you wanna take these two, you're gonna have to go through me," he says, voice low and dangerous, "and I'm not somebody you wanna pick a fight with, Mr. Tresser."

Now Tresser really bristles. It's clear that this situation is getting out of hand, but Henry doesn't have a clue how to stop it. "If you think you can take on the entire Tresser Corporation, you're more stupid than you are naïve. You're harboring Tresser property—"

"I'm *protecting people!*"

"*Property,* because the Tresser agents assigned to this case have legal claim over them. They're not people. They gave up the right to their own identities the moment they died. They're dead, they shouldn't be here now, and they are a danger to themselves and to society."

With each word Tresser speaks, the girl seems to shrink in on herself even further. Beck inches closer to Lehexe, who stares Tresser down with righteous fury burning in his eyes.

"Adam," he says, laying a hand on his friend's shoulder. Lehexe jerks away.

"They're *alive*," he spits, jabbing a finger at Tresser's chest (hopefully no one notices how Henry jumps back). "They ain't your goddamn property, and they ain't dangerous. I'm teaching them how to control themselves. They're not open doors anymore."

"Closed doors. Totally closed," Beck pipes up and looks like he regrets it immediately when all eyes turn to him. "Umm...mostly closed?"

"Almost," the timid girl next to him pipes up. "They can't get in anymore. We're *controlling* it."

"They've been working hard," Lehexe adds. "And their hard work isn't about to fall apart thanks to you."

Tresser's thick eyebrow twitches. He looks more annoyed than Henry has ever seen him; more than that, he looks *angry*. He's the villain in this conversation whether he likes it or not, and he doesn't seem to like it at all.

"What I feel doesn't matter. Corporation policy is that we have to take them in."

The kids shrink back. Lehexe flares up. "You are not taking them anywhere!"

"It's not my choice to make!"

"All right, that's *enough*."

Just when it seems like it's about to get ugly fast, a saving grace steps in. Nathan moves between the two so swiftly, he's like a puzzle piece sliding into place. He snaps the band of tension that has formed between the two, choking off the room's air supply. Suddenly, Henry can breathe again, and Tresser slumps like a puppet whose strings are cut. Lehexe deflates a bit too, still drawn as tightly as a bowstring, but not ready to snap.

Nathan holds out a hand to each combatant, eyes darting between them. He waits until everyone has caught their breath before speaking again. "We're not doing this anymore. We're here for a reason and getting distracted by petty human arguments won't accomplish anything." Tresser opens his mouth to argue, but Nathan doesn't give him the chance. "No one is taking anyone into custody. No one is going anywhere. We're here to speak to Adam Lehexe about the necklace, and that's *all* we're here to do."

"Situation has changed, Nate," Tresser says through gritted teeth. Nathan raises an eyebrow at him.

"Your situation, maybe. Not mine. Our goal is bigger than what you're chasing, Tresser."

"You don't know that—"

Nathan cool glare shuts him up. Henry is a little impressed, and a little frightened. Now he can understand why Nathan is apparently respected so much in his demonic military. He could get babies to stop crying with that look.

Lehexe's wary eyes are fixed on Nathan, growing cooler as the demon turns to him. "I'm sorry about that," he says, and holds out a hand. "Naberos, Knight of the Ninth Quadrant. I represent the Demoniac Alliance here on earth."

Lehexe takes his hand and shakes it with care. "Demoniac Alliance," he echoes. "You're the good guys."

"We are."

"And why're you working with him?" he gestures over his shoulder to Tresser, who bristles. To his credit, Nathan doesn't bat an eye.

"David Tresser and I have formed an alliance to help accomplish the goal of ridding your world of malicious demons." The Tresser Corporation, Henry is starting to gather, is a good ally to have and a bad enemy to make. "He's been a great help so far."

Nathan looks over his shoulder at Tresser, and his lips twitch. It's an obvious olive branch. After a few seconds, the stress fades from Tresser's frown. A bit of the residual tension drains out of his shoulders. He no longer seems as dangerous as he did just minutes ago; now he looks like a child, sulky and disappointed. Henry can tell he wants to say something but is holding his tongue for everyone's sake. Nathan breezes on, unaffected. "We've come to ask for your help. No one will be taking your friends anywhere."

Lehexe nods at Nathan, but then his gaze flickers back over to Tresser. He raises his eyebrows, intent obvious. Tresser scowls until a small hum from Nathan prompts him to chime in with a grumbled, "That's right."

Henry can't help but be amazed. Nathan just humbled David Tresser. He hadn't realized that was *possible.*

Lehexe still looks reluctant, but after a minute spent gauging Nathan's face, his demeanor relaxes. The two workers behind him have shrunk back towards the other side of the counter and look like reluctant observers of a suspense movie—like they wish they could run out of the room, but don't want to miss the show. Henry feels the same way.

"All right," Lehexe says. "What do you need help with?"

Slowly, Henry draws Lucy's amulet from his pocket. Every inch of him is screaming to be cautious, for good reason. He doesn't want to hand the necklace over to a stranger. It would be enough that it's the only clue he has; it's also the closest thing he has left of Lucy. Photos aren't the same, cellphone videos and text conversations, old voicemails and unwashed dishes—none of it is Lucy the way this necklace was. She never took it off.

Giving it to someone else...it feels like Henry is giving away a part of his soul.

But this is for her, he reminds himself. For Lucy. To save her from whatever's happened. If he has to hand over all their savings, their apartment, and his car keys, he'll do it. Anything is worth figuring out where she is.

"This is my fiancée's," he says, passing the necklace to Lehexe. "She's missing. We need to find out where she went."

Lehexe allows the necklace to rest in his open palm. He frowns down at it like he's reading a complicated definition out of a dictionary. His lips trace soundless words. When he looks up at the group, suspicion lines his face. "This necklace has got some impressive protective charms," he declares. "Stronger magic than I'm used to working with. Mostly demon-magic."

Something in Henry's chest leaps. That isn't possible. Lucy didn't use magic; she wasn't a witch. She didn't even like to watch supernatural shows on television; she always called them "too unrealistic".

"What does that mean?"

"If there's a demon nearby, this necklace will let the wearer know. It will keep them from being possessed or harmed by a spirit or demon in any way." He nods to himself. "Impressive magic."

"That doesn't—that doesn't make sense, Lucy wasn't—" Henry feels queasy. "She wasn't a witch."

"You don't have to be a witch to make magic work," Lehexe replies. "You only need to know what you're doing."

"But she wasn't a witch," Henry repeats, as if he needs this point confirmed. Lehexe nods thoughtfully.

"No," he agrees. "From the sort of magic on this necklace, I'd say she was an exorcist."

Henry's entire world seems to shift. It's as if the earth tilts on its axis, just enough to be noticeable but not to throw everything off. Suddenly, colors don't seem quite right, sounds are a little distorted. Everything he thinks he knows is skewed.

Lucy—*his Lucy*. Sweet Lucy, who works in a bookstore, and volunteers at the children's library on weekends? Lucy, who giggles at scary movies, and warbles at the top of her lungs in the shower? Lucy, who has a secret vice for expensive shoes and outfits because they make her "feel fancy"?

Nothing about that woman aligned with Henry's idea of an exorcist. In no way was Lucy similar to David Tresser. She had a happy life, a family...everything she could have wanted. Why on earth would she go chasing after demons?

No. It isn't possible. Lehexe has to be wrong.

"She can't be," he says, moving to snatch the necklace back. Startled, Lehexe jerks backward, and the necklace slips out of his palm. Henry is seized by a flash of blinding fear at the thought of the stones hitting the floor and shattering. Then, another hand snatches it out of thin air.

There is no time to realize it was Beck who rescued the necklace. His pale fingers close around it—and suddenly he goes tense. It is as if he's stuck a fork in an electric socket. He freezes up, eyes going wide, and only has time to gasp before his eyes seem to explode with milky whiteness. They fill up everything, from his cornea to his pupils. It's as startling to see as a demon's black gaze; but even more terrifying is the way all the humanity drains from Beck's expressive face at once.

There is no time to wonder what's going on. "I see her," Beck says in an empty voice.

Henry's pulse picks up. He leans forward, hardly daring to breathe, as Beck's white eyes gape out.

"Chains. Chains around her wrists, her ankles...she's held up against a wall. It's hard to see...it's dark. She's not alone. There's blood, blood, so much blood...she can smell it, feel it, taste it. She's drowning in it." His wide eyes gape at the necklace, unseeing. "It's everywhere. They're dying."

Dying. A sob catches in Henry's throat.

"Where is she?" demands Lehexe. "Do you see that?"

"She's...in prison," the boy mutters. His voice is growing more slurred. "'S dark...not too many guards."

"Why no guards?"

"They can't get out anyway..." he mutters. "No...nothing left. No air. No hope...no life."

"No life?" Henry gasps. Beck's empty eyes turn towards him.

"They're killing her," is all he says, and then the necklace slips from his limp hand.

Beck slumps backwards. Lehexe is immediately there to catch him, wrapping his arms around his waist and bracing them both against the counter to support their weight. It takes a few seconds for Beck to shake off his daze. Humanity returns to his face once again; his eyes uncloud. He stares around at the group for a second, disoriented, before turning back towards Lehexe. "Did...did something happen?"

"Yeah," Tresser says in a tight voice. "The door just cracked open."

Lehexe is worriedly checking Beck over. Beck is quick to reassure him. "I'm okay. I'm okay, Adam, it's fine. Geez, don't look so worried. You see a ghost or something?"

"It's not a joke, Beck," Adam grinds out, but he looks relieved.

Henry can't share in his emotion. His ears are ringing with the fatal portents of Beck's vision. *Blood, and prison, and dying*...it's all his worst fears rolled into one. They're killing Lucy. They're killing Lucy, and she might *already be dead,* and *he can't do anything—*

"Breathe," a low voice sounds near his ear. Henry's wide eyes turn to Nathan, who studies him back with an unreadable expression. "We're going to get to her," Nathan tells him. "You need to keep your head. That's the only way you can help her. Breathe, and know that we'll get there."

Henry does what he says. He breathes.

Filling his lungs is like a breath of relief. The waves of panic crashing over his head begin to recede; as the tide draws back, he's left with more determination than ever. Lucy won't die in a demon prison as long as he can help it.

"This means—" Tresser says, but he has no time to finish. There is a sudden pop behind them. The rich smell of sulfur hits Henry's nose as he is sent sputtering, clamping a hand over his mouth.

"Knight Naberos," an unfamiliar voice says from behind them. "Sorry to interrupt, sir, but it's urgent."

Henry spins around, an exclamation of bewilderment already on his lips, to be met with a man he's never seen before in his life. The figure standing in the middle of Lehexe's shop is dark and well-built, with a serious face and eyes like solid coal. The black smoke swirling around him tells Henry he didn't just step through the front door.

Nathan seems as surprised by the intrusion as anyone but maintains his cool. "Go ahead, Sergeant Valac."

The demon called Valac draws himself up to his full (considerable) height. He looks stressed, Henry realizes for the first time—as if it is *urgent* that he give Nathan this information now, before time runs out. Whatever this is, it's serious. He fights back the urge to groan. The very last thing they need is one more complication, but it's obvious that something has popped up.

"We're gonna need an exorcism fast," Valac says. "We just found him—the first reanimated human, the guy that started this all. We found Matthew Morgan, sir."

Chapter Seven

CASSANDRA SLAMS THE phone down on its receiver. It lands with a sharp clunk that echoes in Malephor's ears and makes her brain feel like it's echoing. As Cassandra braces herself against the coffee table, a heavy sigh tears from her chest.

"You know, most people have cell phones," Malephor remarks.

"That is true," replies Cassandra, sounding tired, "but most people aren't followed around by energy-sapping ghosts 24/7. You know how many times I've tried to make the whole cell phone thing work? Spirits see them as their own personal chargers." Malephor frowns at the rotary phone, which even she can tell is archaic. There's barely even a buzz of energy in it—not enough for spirits to bother with. It might be an inconvenience, but Cassandra figured out how to make do. If Malephor has to guess, she'd say Cassandra probably likes it. It gives her kitchen a cozy, antique sort of feel that seems to fit perfectly with her aesthetic.

Instead of saying any of this, however, Malephor just raises her eyebrows. "I have a cell phone too."

"You do not seem the type," replied Cassandra, lips quirked.

Malephor shrugs. "What did Tresser say?"

"Oh, just his usual fast-talking. Right now, they're bringing my friend Adam over to help with an emergency exorcism of a man who is *supposed* to be dead, but somehow isn't. Oh, also they found Lucy's necklace and need me to figure out where she's been taken. Not to mention, Adam's been housing two recently deceased college students, and Tresser's not thrilled about it. There was probably more, but that's everything I picked up. I couldn't get much in edgewise."

Cassandra breaks off for breath. One hand drags itself through her messy ponytail; she looks exasperated and exhausted, all at once.

Malephor's bares her fangs. "The man has no sense of tact."

Cassandra catches her eye, and some of the tension in her face fades away. Just for emphasis, Malephor curls her lips back a bit more. Any other human would draw back at something so nonhuman, monstrous. Cassandra is different. Malephor knows it isn't as if Cassandra is more used to demons. She isn't unafraid. Cassandra is human, and all humans are scared of monsters.

Cassandra looks at Malephor, however, and doesn't seem to see a monster at all.

"If you want to bite him, feel free," she hums, reaching across the counter to drag a pen and pad of paper towards her. Her brows furrow as she scribbles on it. "Just don't take off anything important."

"Deal." Malephor leaves the table and peers over her shoulder. Cassandra has very spindly handwriting. It's hard to make out her letters, almost as if she's writing in code—thankfully, Malephor has experience with codes. She studies the short list for a moment before figuring out that it's not a secret message, and Cassandra just has really sloppy handwriting.

"I'm going to need your help, Mal."

She's immediately at attention. "Anything."

Cassandra doesn't smile this time. She's too busy frowning down at the paper, like it's filled with answers but too stubborn to give them up to her. After a second, she huffs, nodding to herself. "Okay, I need you to go down to the basement. Second door on the left, down the hall. There's a box of beeswax candles, and we're going to need all of them. And chalk. The box of chalk is on the wooden shelf... I think I have a chalice there too. That could be useful. I'll get the holy water and incense, and the herb bundles..."

"Herb bundles?" Malephor's brain fights to keep up with the onslaught of information. "For what?"

"Burning, of course." Cassandra blinks at her like it ought to be obvious.

"Of course."

Malephor descends to the basement as asked and finds herself in a crowded storage area. Cassandra's basement seems well-stocked with everything she could possibly need—a treadmill in the corner of the room, covered with storage bags of winter clothing, a half-assembled IKEA desk, old cardboard boxes, Christmas decorations, and rows of shelves lining the far wall. These shelves are the highlight of the room. They're stacked tightly with boxes of candles, bags and containers of herbs, old crystals, and the occasional book. It looks like a witch's paradise.

Tentatively, Malephor scans through the book titles. Cassandra doesn't have any spellbooks. The volumes she does have are all to do with communicating with spirits: *The Rite of Exorcism, Protecting Your Space, Ghosts and Their Origins, A Guide to Spirit Banishment.* It seems like Cassandra has all the information she could need at her fingertips.

Then again, nothing educated quite like experience. Cassandra certainly has a lot of that as well.

Tentatively, Malephor pulls one of the books down from the shelf. It's not that she's interested in banishing spirits; the feeling of the book in her hand is what thrills her. Back home, they don't have books. Demons have little use for reading, no reason or time. The military uses couriers to deliver important messages, and paperwork is filed by sergeants assigned to oversee the barrier. Real books? With spines and pages, chapters and titles? The demon world has nothing like it.

Malephor cracks open the book. Her hands run along the edges of the pages, feeling them flutter against her fingertips.

It's *beautiful*.

"Mal, did you find them?"

Cassandra stops at the top of the stairs when she spots Malephor holding the book. She seems surprised, but only for a moment.

"I've heard of books before," Malephor says. She saw them too, upstairs among Cassandra's well-stocked bookshelves. "But I've never held one before."

"Never?" Cassandra's nose crinkles. The stairs creak as she takes a few more steps down. "Here, we have whole libraries—buildings *full* of books. The library is one of my favorite places in town. I can't imagine never holding a book."

Malephor blinks down at the cover. "I think I like it."

"How about..." When she looks up, there's a light dancing in Cassandra's eyes. It is as brilliant as the glow of the Pits in Quadrant Four, the same ones Malephor grew up with; but it carries none of the foreboding. Cassandra's eyes are full of warmth. "Once this is all over, you can pick out some books? Any ones you want, from my shelves. You can take them with you?"

Slowly, Malephor smiles. "I would like that very much."

She finds the candles with Cassandra's help, and together they lug all the material up to Cassandra's parlor. The room is still cluttered with furniture. Cassandra sighs, puts her hands on her hips, and surveys it. "All right. Mal, do you think you could pull the table—"

Malephor doesn't say a word. She just braces herself and charges forward. In a matter of minutes, all the furniture—from the couches and chairs to the great oak coffee table—has been moved to the far sides of the room, leaving a great empty space in the center.

"Oh." Cassandra seems surprised. "All right. Cool."

After that, Malephor lets Cassandra take the lead. There's not much she can do, anyway. She hasn't studied these things the way Cassandra has; she doesn't know the intricacies of an exorcism ritual. She watches Cassandra sketch a chalk circle on her hardwood floor with interest.

It is a wide, closed off circle, with a second ring inside of it. Inside of that ring, Cassandra sketches a long-limbed pentagram. When she moves on to the layer of the circle, her chalk-covered hands begin to move rapidly. She inscribes spindly symbols, all looping handwriting and careful lines. They are foreign, but not, all at once. They are familiar. They are nerve-wracking. Malephor swears she has seen these symbols before in a dream, or a nightmare.

It feels wrong to be witnessing all of this. She's a *demon*. She knows she has no reason to feel threatened by Cassandra's preparations herself, but should she be helping set up an exorcism? Putting aside the fact that they're exorcizing a Legion soldier...it seems wrong for Malephor to be doing this. She can't explain it, but it makes her uncomfortable.

Perhaps she isn't as subtle as she believes, because Cassandra notices. She pauses as she adjusts a wooden chair in the center of the circle. Her eyes lock on Malephor, and she frowns. "Are you okay? You don't have to be here, if you'd rather not."

She doesn't want to be here—but the idea that she *ought* to leave causes Malephor's old stubbornness to flare up. She isn't weak. She isn't vulnerable. She can't have Cassandra thinking otherwise. "No," she answers promptly. "I'm staying."

"Are you sure?"

Malephor doesn't dignify this with a reply. After a few seconds, Cassandra sighs. Her eyes drift to a bundle of rope sitting on the outside of the circle. She takes a step towards it, but Malephor gets there first.

She only manages to wrap one hand around the ropes before drawing back with a sharp hiss. The flesh of her palm sizzles; rotten sulfur fills the air. Cassandra springs forward, plucking the ropes up before they can hit the ground.

"*Sorry,* sorry, you can't touch those. They're consecrated. If a demon tugs on them, they'll burn up..." She discards the armful of ropes in the center of the circle, and spins back to Malephor. Her hands flutter at her sides; she seems uncertain of what to do, but eager to do something. "Are you okay?"

"Great," Malephor mutters between gritted teeth. She's had much worse.

Cassandra is silent for a moment. Malephor is too occupied with her scorched skin to notice until the human speaks up in a very soft voice. "Please don't do that."

Malephor glances up at her. Cassandra's golden brow furrows in frustration. "Don't lie to me. Don't keep saying things are 'great' or 'okay' or 'fine', when they aren't. I don't...I don't know *why* you do it, but you don't have to. I want you to be happy, Mal."

"I am happy." It's not a lie; she isn't unhappy.

"Comfortable, then. I want you to feel like you can be honest with me."

Slowly, Cassandra reaches out and takes Malephor's hand in her own. Her pale fingers glance along the burn; Malephor can't help hissing. Cassandra catches this and raises her eyebrows.

"You don't have to lie," she says again. Then she pulls on Malephor's arm. "Come on. I've got something to take care of this."

She allows Cassandra to lead her down carpeted hallways, past open and closed doors, paintings of landscapes and tiny mirrors hanging on the walls. Malephor's eyes wander to each one. She is intensely interested in her surroundings, maybe to avoid looking at Cassandra.

Cassandra's bathroom is monochrome, almost antique. She has a claw-foot bathtub, which reminds Malephor of something she'd see back home. A vibrant cascade of crystals hang in the corner of the room, catching the fluorescent lights and making them dance along the shower walls. Looking at the display makes Malephor dizzy. She tries to study the black-and-white pattern of the floor tiles instead.

Cassandra ushers her over the edge of the bathtub and urges her to sit. Malephor does so. She twists a knob nearest to her, and blinks as water escapes the silver faucet. When she twists it back, the water dies in the faucet's slender throat. Plumbing is a little human revolution that demons would have no need of but is endlessly interesting. It is awfully funny how humans are able to make something remarkable out of nothing, Malephor thinks.

Cassandra throws open the mirrored cabinet and pulls down a clear bottle, filled with something bright pink. Malephor immediately distrusts anything so neon and bares her teeth when Cassandra turns back to her. The human only shakes her head, shaking the bottle along with it. "It's just calamine lotion. Homemade. Don't be a baby."

Malephor is anything but. She sets her jaw and leans forward, holding out her hand. She's endured hellfire and taken on a High Demon. There is nothing scary about a bottle of medicine.

Cassandra smiles. "Atta girl."

Her hand still pulses with pain, radiating right down to the bone. Her skin is an ugly, blistered red; it bubbles like it's ready to burst at any second. Just looking at it makes Malephor queasy, and she's been known to have a strong stomach. Cassandra doesn't flinch, however. She just takes Malephor's hand in her own gentle as a butterfly touch and spreads a bit of the mixture on her palm.

The lotion is cool. Malephor hisses instinctively but doesn't pull away. It brings the agonizing pulse of her hand down, making it almost bearable. She doesn't want to escape the relief. She needs more of it.

Cassandra notices the look on her face, and chuckles. Malephor dislikes being laughed at. When she looks at Cassandra, though, it couldn't be more obvious that she isn't amused by *her*. Malephor presses her hand up as Cassandra continues to massage the lotion into it, and

Cassandra hums to herself as she spreads more. The swelling is going down. The bubbles on Malephor's skin begin to shrink, as if they were never there at all. It's a miracle potion.

Magic, Malephor's brain supplies. She tries not to be derisive, though she can't help it. Humans take advantage of magic when they have it, yet are quick to forget (or deny) that it exists. Any human power pales in comparison to demonic abilities, but Cassandra... Cassandra just might have the hang of this magic thing.

It is a long moment before Cassandra speaks. Until then, the quiet was so absolute that Malephor is startled.

"What's your home like? Is it a nice place?"

She's not accusing Malephor of being a liar again, at least. Still, Malephor stares at her. "It's Hell."

Cassandra continues to blot the lotion across Malephor's palm. She doesn't blink. "Okay. Not so nice?"

Malephor considers this for a moment before shrugging. "It's home."

"What about family? You must have some of that, right? Or...or friends?"

The edge of curiosity in Cassandra's tone threatens to overpower it. It is like a tide churning just beneath the surface of her words. Whatever innocence they might have contained is swept away. Malephor isn't used to people asking questions about her and doesn't know how to react. There's no reason to lie. Telling the truth only seems strange because she's never told anyone her history before; she's never wanted to or been asked.

"No family," she answers slowly. "Demons are not like humans. We aren't born—we just begin to exist as if we always have. We have...mentors who we learn from. Not parents."

Cassandra's head bobs along to Malephor's words—though she refrains from the irritating human habit of *humming* to make it clear that she's listening. Her ponytail sways behind her, like strands of raw wheat falling against her back. Her face is shamelessly curious now; her eyes bore into Malephor like a puzzle.

"I don't have friends," Malephor continues. "I'm not...not..."

Cassandra opens her mouth, but Malephor abruptly can't stand the idea of needing to be helped. "A friend person," she finishes. It's a painfully human colloquialism. It makes Cassandra smile in spite of herself.

"Well, if it makes you feel better, neither am I." She gives one final dab at Malephor's hand before leaning back. "Besides, I always say three great friends are better than three hundred good ones."

"Or just one." When Cassandra looks up at her, Malephor holds her gaze. "Just one."

She smiles. "I'm glad to be your first friend, Mal."

When Cassandra pulls her hands away, the absence of touch stings worse than the rope burn. Still, Malephor holds on to that secret little smile, and decides it's okay. She has a friend; a *human* friend.

And she couldn't imagine any better friend to have than Cassandra Carlyle.

THE CIRCLE RESTS in the center of the floor, surrounded by a ring of ivory candles. Five candles, each sitting at a central point of the pentagram. Bundles of herbs line the walls, ready to be set alight. The sigils lining the floors are to dance whenever Malephor looks at them.

Cassandra's careful work stands out starkly, iridescent white against the dark floor.

It would not be pleasant to be exorcized, Malephor decides. Even if Cassandra were the one doing it.

They've just finished laying salt lines on all the windows and back doors when the sound of an engine sputtering up Cassandra's long driveway reaches them.

Cassandra drops what she's doing and wipes down her hands. When she peers out the nearest curtained window, she has to stand on her toes.

"That'd be the cavalry," Cassandra announces. She flashes Malephor an enigmatic little smile, red lips twisting in a way that makes her whole face look prettier than before. Given Cassandra's general prettiness, this is an achievement. "Are we ready?"

Forcing her face to remain neutral, Malephor shrugs. "As we'll ever be."

"Good." Cassandra claps her hands, smooths down her dress, and smiles. "Let's hope this isn't a disaster."

Chapter Eight

CASSANDRA IS A little alarmed when Tresser comes barging into her house toting not just the party of Nathan and Henry, but what seems like an entire clown-car full of people. She really has no clue how everyone fit into the hearse.

A disgruntled-looking Henry stumbles out first, followed by what seems to be an endless stream of visitors. Adam slips out of the vehicle, silent and graceful as a phantom. He's followed closely by Alyssa, who trails after him like an anxious child clinging to a parent's arm. Then Beck trips out of the car, only to be caught by Adam's quick hand. After them comes someone Cassandra has never even seen before—a muscular, severe-looking man carrying someone else, who's either unconscious or dead.

Cassandra's life has always been weird, but these past few days have just been *too* weird.

"Hope you've got your cross and bible out," Tresser remarks as the entire troupe files into Cassandra's house. She doesn't get a chance to snap back before the other man is gone, so she settles for rolling her eyes instead. She thinks no one notices until she catches Malephor's smirk.

Nathan actually has the decency to pull her aside and brief her in more explicit detail than Tresser. Cassandra's first question is, "Can I ask about the unconscious guy?"

"That would be Matt Morgan," Nathan replies, glancing towards where his two demon Sergeants are setting up Matt in the middle of Cassandra's living room. "Sergeant Valac's platoon located him in a cemetery on Madison Street. According to them, he was kneeling over one of the graves and doing something to it."

"Doing what, exactly?"

"Good question. If he's the first reanimated human, he could be the key to all the rest of them."

"You don't think he's the one bringing people back?"

Nathan stares at her for a silent moment. He doesn't have an answer. There's no way of knowing for sure just how Matt is tied to people like Beck and Alyssa. Just thinking about it makes a sense of foreboding swell in Cassandra's chest.

Her gaze is pulled to where Beck and Alyssa sit in one corner of the room, spread across the couch. Beck is watching intently as Adam studies the exorcism circle, commenting here and there in a voice too low for anyone but Adam to hear. Alyssa is silent, but Henry is sitting next to her and chattering. He's trying to coax her out of her shell, and it's working, a bit—she smiles at one of his jokes.

They're good kids. The last thing Cassandra wants is to see them get hurt. If Matt Morgan can answer the question of why people are coming back from the dead...

Well, they'd better get this exorcism right, then.

With the help of Tresser, Valac finishes securing Matt to the kitchen chair (tying him down seems a bit extreme, but Cassandra values her furniture too much to argue) and straightens up. There is a tight look on his face; his jaw is set like it's been wired shut, and his eyes have gone full-black. He stalks up to Nathan, the picture of stiff formality, and salutes.

"Job's done, sir. I have to get back to my squad."

"Thank you, Sergeant Valac. Excellent work."

A flash of movement behind Valac focuses Cassandra's attention on George. She's taken aback by the look the ghost wears; never before has she seen such a melancholy expression on George's face. His mischievousness has vanished, replaced by what almost looks like shell-shock. He reaches out, brushing his fingers over the back of Valac's neck, and the demon's stiffness splinters as a shiver courses through him.

Valac's eyes widen, and his discomfort doubles. With one last muttered farewell to Nathan, he vanishes from the room.

"Jesus," George mutters. He sounds more shaken than Cassandra has ever heard him—breathless. Which is quite a feat, considering ghosts don't breathe. "Call me crazy, but I think he could feel me."

Cassandra watches the small quaver in his jaw, as if he wants to say something else but is holding himself back. It's so unlike George that she can't help her bafflement. "You know him?"

George's attention snaps back to her, as if he's just remembered Cassandra exists. "No," he says quickly. "Nah, never seen him before."

That's typical George—shutting down whenever the conversation gets personal. Cassandra would be a liar if she said she wasn't itching with curiosity, but she knows better than to push.

Instead, she turns her attention back to the circle. It looks as perfect as they're going to get it; she and Malephor set up well. Of course, that's no guarantee that everything will go smoothly. She's done this enough times that she has the rites memorized and the exorcism sigils engraved in her head. Still, she can't help the thrill of nerves that courses through her when she looks at Matt, bound to the chair with his limp head bowed.

Exorcisms are always an experience, but Cassandra has the inexplicable feeling that this one will be unlike any other. There's a low churn of anxiety in the pit of her stomach. She's not used to feeling nervous before an exorcism. She'd be lying if she said it didn't set her on edge.

"I don't like this."

She jumps at the sudden voice next to her. Malephor has reappeared, as if out of thin air; (maybe literally—she's a demon, after all). Now she has her arms crossed, surveying the scene with skepticism. Her eyebrows quirk as her gaze flickers over to Cassandra. "What do you think?"

Cassandra shrugs and sighs. "I think in this room we have two experienced exorcists, two demonic warriors, and an agent of the foremost organization for relations between human and demonkind. However, this could go wrong, we're as prepared as we can get."

Malephor's gaze lingers on her for a moment longer before drifting back to the circle. She doesn't look pleased but offers no more arguments.

Whatever Valac did to knock his target out seems to be wearing off. Matt is beginning to stir, head shifting and a small moan emitting from his throat. It'll take him a few moments to regain consciousness, but this is it. Cassandra's breath feels short with anticipation.

"Hey, Adam..." Beck suddenly lurches forward, pressing a hand to his head. His face screws up in discomfort. He looks queasy as he sways in place. "I'm not feelin' too great..."

Next to him, Alyssa has taken on a similar faint expression. She is breathing hard, looking seconds away from fainting, and Cassandra inches forward, ready to catch her in case she does. They're both looking to Adam as if he has all the answers, but Adam just frowns back at them with an expression of baffled worry.

"Go downstairs, Beck," he says after a few seconds. "The both of you. Get some air."

Henry stands up unexpectedly, laying a hand on both Beck and Alyssa's arms and pulling their attention from their bemused protector. "C'mon, kids. I got a look at Cassie's coffee maker this morning. Let's see if I remember how to use it!"

"He's gonna blow that thing up," George snickers from his perch on top of the coffee table.

As Henry leads the duo out of the room, Cassandra feels her heart sink. She lives off of coffee, and the last thing she needs is to find her two-hundred-dollar machine reduced to scrap metal by whatever Henry can think to do to it. Knowing his luck, Henry will short-circuit the thing, or actually manage to blow it to pieces.

"Cheer up, Cassie. You've still got a microwave."

Cassandra shoots George a glare. "What?" demands the ghost. "You've never microwaved coffee before?"

"I'm really disgusted right now," Cassandra mutters. "And disappointed in you."

George shoots her a wink that has Cassandra rolling her eyes and turning her back on the ghost. Malephor raises an eyebrow; Cassandra just shrugs and nods over her shoulder. She doesn't have to say anything else for Malephor's head to bob in understanding. It's a nice change from the reaction she usually gets - bafflement, followed by no small amount of confusion, and a little concern. There's a reason Cassandra has gotten so good at hiding her gifts.

Another groan from Matt pulls everyone's attention back to him, and he raises his head. Cassandra's back straightens, and she recites the exorcism incantation in her mind. Adam moves forward, blessed water in one hand and chalk in the other. He's only taken a few steps forward, however, when he stops dead in his tracks.

Cassandra hears Tresser inhale an audible breath. Next to him, Nathan has gone stiff. Adam looks utterly bemused, and Malephor's frown has deepened. All Cassandra can focus on is one thing—the ordinary hazel eyes of the young man in the circle. Matt Morgan—the *real* Matt Morgan—looks between them all with hazy confusion.

"W-wait...what?" his voice comes out clear, unencumbered by demonic influence. "What's going on?"

For a moment, everyone is silent. Nathan finally speaks up. "Can you tell us your name, sir?"

Matt's frown grows a bit more uncertain. He looks confused, vulnerable, and very, very human. "It's Matt...what's happening?"

Cassandra's frown deepens. She exchanges a glance with Adam. This is a turn of events they hadn't anticipated, and now neither one is sure what their next step should be. Demons *can't lie* about their names. If Matt is able to say he's Matt, that means he's the one in control. That doesn't make sense. Cassandra can still feel the demonic energy clinging to him, wrapped so tightly around his being that it could easily smother him. He's not just carrying around residual energy, he's possessed. There's no reason for him to be in control right now.

Unless...

"Wait, so he's *not* possessed?" demands George, so close to Cassandra's ear that she can't help flinching. "I thought Jack said there was a demon in this guy!"

There *is*, if Cassandra is right. One look at Adam tells him that he's thinking exactly the same thing.

Something is inside of Matt Morgan. If they want to stand any chance at helping him, they have to draw it out.

Matt's eyes are darting around the room, wide and frightened. He tries to move, only to be held in place by the rope that restrains him. An alarmed yelp tears from his throat as he realizes he's tied down.

Adam hastily scrawls a sigil on Matt's forehead in chalk marker, then another on his chest. Cassandra takes a deep breath and begins to recite, *"Immundu spiritus potestatem invoco—"*

"What are you doing?" exclaims Matt.

"Cessa decipere humanas creaturas—"

A sudden convulsion wracks Matt's body. It's a spasm, almost too quick to notice, but just for a second his eyes flash black. Then he's back to himself, writhing at the bonds with new urgency. Ragged breaths cause his chest to heave against the confines of the rope. The muscles in his arms strain as he struggles to free them from behind his back, rubbing his wrists raw in the process.

"Please," he gasps. "Please don't, please, don't let it come back, *don't* —"

He is crazed with fear. It makes Cassandra's stomach churn as she feels Matt's energy begin to be overpowered by the demon's own.

(This isn't what she does. She helps people. She doesn't force their bodies out of their control. This is so wrong...)

"Please," Matt gasps, choking on a sob. "I want—home—don't bring him back—please!"

Cassandra squeezes her eyes shut.

"Ergo, draco maledicte et omnis legio diabolica, adjuramus te!"

*(She **is** helping Matt. This is the only way.)*

Matt's head snaps back in a guttural scream. No sooner has it broken from his throat than he is wracked by sudden, violent convulsions. His head thrashes back and forth, a distorted blur on quaking shoulders. His back twists into a spine-snapping arch. The screech he emits sends a sharp burst of agony shooting through Cassandra's head.

Then, just as suddenly as it began, everything goes silent.

Matt's head slumps forward and slowly raises. He regards them with inky black eyes.

"Okay, that worked," Tresser mutters.

It worked a little *too* well. Matt's lips curl back in a terrible rictus grin; teeth gleam in his gaping mouth like spearheads. His tongue flickers out to brush over dry lips, and Cassandra feels his awful gaze slide over her.

"Well," he says. "This is some party."

Nathan's entire body has gone rigid, and a tension radiates from him that sets Cassandra's nerves on edge. Malephor is her own brand of agitation; she stands very still, arms crossed over her chest, glowering. Tresser has a knife in one fist, knuckles tight around the hilt, while his other hand grips the back of the nearest chair.

The air in the room has grown dense and heavy. Shadows lengthen to fill every corner, suffocating any light they come across. The room is as dark as Matt's eyes, dark as the terrible grin that distorts his face, and when he laughs, the sound seems to burst throughout the room like a string of firecrackers.

"Nice of you to invite me in," the demon says. "I would never have gotten through the wards otherwise. Very hospitable of you, Cassandra Carlyle."

Cassandra feels her blood turn to ice in her veins. Malephor's eyes dart over, catching hers for a split second. She looks ready to spring forward, but Cassandra steels herself and returns the demon's wicked gaze.

"I let you in my house for one reason," she says. "To banish you."

"Banish me? Not kill me?" Matt sneers. "You don't believe in killing demons. Not with your *abilities*. Killing something would just make one more dead thing hanging over your head." He gives a guttural laugh. "What if I killed this body right now? Made his heart explode in his chest? Would you feel that, Cassandra? Would you kill me then?"

Cassandra can't help the way she shrinks back, the demon's words getting under her skin in the worst way. She can't stomach the thought of harm coming to Matt just so the demon can prove a point to her. Where Cassandra steps away, Malephor steps forward.

"She wouldn't kill you," replies Malephor in a low snarl, "but I would. Don't hurt that man."

"When do *you* care about humans, Knight of the Fourth Quadrant? Oh, sorry—that should be Sergeant. You're not a High Demon." Matt grins again, teeth like bullets. "Not like I am. A word of advice: you'll never get anywhere with that attitude. Fondness for your pet human will only hold you back. But you know that, of course. What do you want more, to keep her or to grow stronger? Now, if you turned around and just slashed her pretty little throat—"

Malephor lunges forwards. Only Cassandra's grip on her arm keeps her from tearing Matt to pieces. When the demon rounds on her, Cassandra's heart leaps at the rage blazing in Malephor's eyes; but, slowly, that fire quells down to embers. Malephor keeps her eyes trained on Cassandra for several long seconds until she's able to breathe again. Only then does Cassandra feel safe letting her go.

It's impossible for this demon to know so much about them all—their names, details, inner thoughts. It must have a way of knowing. Cassandra wracks her brain to understand how. High Demons are always powerful, but some demons are endowed with their own special abilities. Some can shapeshift; others can fly; some can snake their way into minds...

"Bingo." Matt's demon smirks at her, and Cassandra feels queasy.

"He's in our heads," she announces to the group. "He's able to read our minds."

"That's great," Tresser retorts. He sounds more annoyed than alarmed. When the demon's eyes turn to him, he doesn't shrink back. "My brain is a booze-soaked mess of debauchery, self-loathing, and showtunes. Try me."

They don't have time for this. *"Impius spiritus, exorcizamus te—"* Cassandra begins; but when the demon's gaze swerves to her she finds her voice frozen in her throat.

She tries to choke past it but can't. She can't speak, she can't *breathe—*

"In nomine Domini et beatus mundi," Adam speaks up, continuing where Cassandra left off. When Matt's attention flickers to him, Cassandra is able to breathe once more. *"Et abierunt—"*

"You're angry," the demon hisses, sounding thrilled. "You've lost so much already, and now they want to take away the only good thing you have left?"

Adam doesn't falter. *"Cessa decipere humanas—"*

"You lost your grandparents. Saw your father die. You cut yourself off from the family you had left. You lost *your best friend.* All because of magic."

"Et revertatur ad te mundi diabolica. Hic non receperint vos—"

"So you're ready to destroy anyone who tries to take what you still have. Do you really think you're that strong? Do you really think you can protect him?"

"Ut mittatur foras, te rogamus—"

"From what's inside of him? From *himself?"*

"Audi nos!"

The final words of the incantation ring out with finality. A dead silence falls across the room. Matt looks around at them and grins.

"You don't have the power," he says, and the dining room table goes flying across the room.

It smashes just over Cassandra's shoulder; a gasp freezes in her throat. The demon rolls his shoulders and leans back, stretching his arms out in both sides of him; the ropes binding him unfurl in midair. Slowly, he rises to his feet, studying his frozen interrogators.

Until that point everyone had been doing a pretty good job of not panicking. Now, it's a challenge not to. He has been *toying* with them the entire time. The circle has no ability to hold him. The ropes are doing nothing. There is a demon loose in Cassandra's house, and their exorcism has had no effect on him.

They've been playing the demon's game all along.

Cassandra's first instinct is to hit the ground, but she forces past her fear and takes a step closer to Matt. One of the framed pictures on the wall flies at her head. She just manages to duck, avoiding the smiling face of her father by inches. Another photo flies forward, but Malephor snatches it out of the air seconds before it can hit Cassandra's temple.

Tresser rolls head over heels as the ropes snap out at him. A handful of salt goes flying at the demon. It smokes off of his skin, but if it causes Matt pain, he doesn't show it. Instead, he just sneers and flings a chair Tresser's way, knocking him flat with the impact.

"Is this how you're hoping to impress your father? You're *really* making the Tresser Corporation proud! Think about it, David, when has he ever been proud of you? When has he ever loved you like a father *should—*"

There is a horrible crash as the demon's chair slams into his back, sending him sprawling to the ground. Stunned, Matt struggles to get to his feet; but he does not have the chance before Nathan stalks across the room and seizes him by his shoulders, hauling him upright. Residual energy still radiates off of Nathan from the pulse that sent the chair flying, but there is no time for Cassandra to question how he did it.

"Don't look at him," Nathan orders in a dangerous voice. "Look at me."

Matt grins again. "Ahh, you're Naberos. Everyone's heard of you. You're the one they call The Demoniac Alliance's Greatest Weapon. You've finally got your own unit, isn't that right?"

Nathan doesn't flinch, though his eyes fill with pitch blackness. "Where have you taken the people you stole?"

"Now you want answers?" Matt spits. "Who says I'll give them to you?"

"Where?" Nathan demands again, not flinching. Cassandra catches sight of crimson blooming against the white of Matt's T-shirt. Sharp claws dig into his skin where Nathan has a deadlock on his shoulders.

This actually gets the demon to grimace. "They're exactly where you think they would be," he snarls. "*The Pits of Gehenna*—the greatest prison in all of Hell."

"What are you doing to them there?"

Matt's lips curl in a catlike grin. "There are people who are terrified of you. Allies on your own side don't trust you. How can you be sure the men under you are loyal? You're only their leader for one reason, and they know what it is."

Whether Nathan realizes it or not, his fingers tighten on Matt's shoulders. As his nails bury themselves in vulnerable flesh, Matt's smile grows even more twisted and desperate. "They've always been terrified of you! You're a weapon. You've only *ever* been a weapon. Do you really think becoming a war hero change that?"

"What are they doing to the people?" Nathan demands again. Matt cackles.

"Wouldn't you like to know... *Interitus.*"

When Matt spits in his face, the sound echoes in the dead silent room. Nathan drops him to the floor and steps back, swiping the insult off his cheek. Matt sneers at him. Malephor takes a step forward, but Nathan holds up an arm to warn her back.

"We will storm the Pits of Gehenna to free them," he says, staring down the demon at his feet. "I will be there the moment the Righteous Legion sees its end, and your every word, everything you and your comrades have done, will mean nothing. I may be destruction, but you and your kind are *nothing.*"

The insult strikes home. Cassandra sees it in the shift of Matt's face, from audacious glee to pure rage. She sees it in Matt's bared teeth, the glass-cut line of his jaw. She feels it in the spike of energy in the air as it steals her breath.

One second later, chaos erupts.

Nathan drops to the ground as a massive wave of force explodes outwards, sending everything in its path airborne. Cassandra is on her feet, and then she is not.

The bodies fly—one, two, three, like drops of rain in the middle of a storm. Cassandra is flung headfirst into the couch; Adam hits the coffee table with a wood-splintering crash, and Tresser hurtles into the farthest wall of the room.

His body connects with an awful sound. When he crumples to the floor, he does not get up again.

For a moment, there is silence. Cassandra's ears are ringing, and she cannot hear anything at all. She cannot hear the taunts that spew from the gaping, warped wound that is Matt Morgan's mouth. She cannot hear the panicked yell of Tresser's name that bursts past Nathan's lips. She cannot hear Malephor's voice, even though she is right over her, grasping her tight and pulling her back up.

Only when her feet are on solid ground do things become real again. Everything rushes back.

"Are you okay?" Malephor is repeating, louder and louder, in her ear. "Cassandra, answer me!"

Cassandra opens her mouth, but her words are stolen by the flash of Nathan's eyes. They tear away from the crumpled form of Tresser and lock upon Matt. Once clear as the country sky, his eyes are now electric—bright blue and blazing. Lightning illuminates his pupils as they pulse with pure energy. Utter fury twists his face; rage mixed with something lethal. He rises to his feet once more.

When Nathan explodes, the breath that had been stalled in Cassandra's throat releases all at once. The light is blinding, and it burns when it washes over her. It is energy in its purest form, raw and uninhibited. She feels it pulse over her skin and cannot help the way her knees buckle. Eyes slide shut automatically against the onslaught of brightness. She feels her hands pressing against her face but does not have the strength to pull away. At least this way she is given some protection from the *screaming.*

Matt roars like a dying animal as the demon inside him is sucked out all at once. It is quick and easy—like a vacuum, pulling out every speck of poison. The demonic energy flies out of him, and Cassandra feels the dense pulse of it in open air for just a second before that explodes too. Suddenly the demon is no more, and there is a lot more air in the room.

When Cassandra opens her eyes, she finds Nathan on his knees. Hands press against his sweat-soaked forehead; his chest heaves. Every movement seems forced, painful, drawn out of him by some strength of will that is quickly running low. In front of Nathan, Matt is slumped in the chair. A thin trickle of blood runs from his nose, but he is otherwise limp. Cassandra narrows her eyes at him and heaves a sigh when she feels no trace of demonic energy.

Matt is cleansed. *Somehow,* against every odd, it worked.

How?

"Tresser." Despite the fatigue obvious in every inch of his body, Nathan drags himself across the floor to Tresser's side. "Wake up. Tresser, come on."

He pulls Tresser's dark head into his lap, and it is only a second before Tresser stirs. A groan tears from his parted lips. He blinks blearily up at Nathan for a moment before heaving a breathless laugh.

"You look like you've seen better days."

The smile that breaks across Nathan's face is like the sun breaking through a barrier of clouds. "Thanks a lot," he huffs. "So do you."

It doesn't make sense. Nothing else they tried worked. No sigils, no incantations, no spells were able to exorcise whatever inhabited Matt's body. Yet Nathan did it using nothing but his own energy.

It should be impossible. If Cassandra hadn't seen it herself, she wouldn't believe it. Surely *no one* could be that powerful...

She finds herself by Matt's side as soon as she's back on her feet. She paws at the young man's face, lifting his head and brushing back his bangs. Her hope is to wake him, but it's no use. His face is slack, as if he's sleeping, and his mouth hangs slightly open. Dark purple bruises rim his eyes. His skin is ice-cold to the touch.

He's very...very cold.

Cassandra's heart is suddenly in her throat as she fumbles for a pulse. There is none. She presses her ear to Matt's chest and can hear no heartbeat, no breath. Nothing. Morbid, endless silence.

As a last resort, Cassandra strains to find Matt's lifeline—the little thread of energy that runs through everyone, always pulsing, always vibrant. She has to fight for it; like swimming through molasses, her every effort weighed down by dead energy. When she finally locates it, it burns like a dying flame—growing smaller and smaller with every second.

"No," Cassandra breathes, and scrambles to grasp Matt's lifeline. If she could strengthen it, if she could help it burn brighter, help Matt *stay alive*...

It flickers out before she can so much as touch it.

Cassandra falls back, stunned. Her entire body feels hollowed out. As her hands slip out of Matt's own, the young man's body slumps forward again. There is nothing left in him now. No energy. No life.

"Is he—" Tresser says but cuts himself off. He exhales a deep sigh.

Cassandra just has time to register Malephor's hand fall upon her shoulder before a crash echoes from the next room. It is earthshaking. The shatter of glass rings in Cassandra's ears. Not a second later a shout bellows out, and all at once she feels as if the breath has been sucked out of her.

"Beck!" Adam hollers and takes off. He knows. Maybe he can feel it, the same way Cassandra can feel the pain radiating through every cell in her body. Down in his soul, Adam knows.

The rest of the room is one step behind him, Malephor tugging Cassandra up when she makes no move to rise to her feet. They rush into the kitchen to find Henry standing in the middle of the room. Crouched on the counter, George looks stunned, gaping at the scene before him. The other two occupants of the room are very still.

Beck lies crumpled next to a shattered coffee mug. He is on his side, motionless, face slack as if he were only sleeping. His chest is still; his energy is gone.

Alyssa sits slumped at the kitchen table with her head buried in her arms. Hair hangs in her face, but Cassandra knows that she too would wear an empty, lifeless expression.

Adam hits the floor at Beck's side. His arms are around him, pulling him into his lap, before anyone else can even think about moving forward. His face is twisted in agony. "Beck? *Beck*...wake up. C'mon Beck, wake up…don't do this, don't leave me, *don't…*"

He's scrambling to look for an injury, searching Beck's head and chest for wounds, but there are none to be found. There's nothing Adam can do.

At Alyssa's side, Nathan is pale as a ghost. He has the girl in his arms when he slowly shakes his head.

They're gone. They're all gone.

"I didn't see what…they were fine, they were okay and talking and then they just collapsed…" Henry sounds breathless, close to tears as he hovers around Alyssa's body. "What the hell *happened?*"

"Beck, come on! *Wake up!*" Adam's voice breaks on the last word. To Cassandra's horror, she realizes that her friend is weeping. Silent sobs wrack his chest, while tears drop from his eyes onto Beck's cold face.

In the middle of it all, Cassandra finds herself gripping Malephor's arm to keep upright. Such a sudden onslaught of sorrow and death has her woozy. She can *feel* it—every ounce of pain, the emptiness that comes with the life draining out of someone threefold. She can feel all of it, and it's strangling her. She doesn't think she can stand to be in this room anymore. She can't look at the bodies. She can't watch Adam weep. She can't see Nathan staring down at his hands, slow horror dawning on his face.

"Did I…" Nathan starts, then takes a deep breath. "Did I do this?"

Tresser stares at him hard but doesn't reply. Nobody says a word. Nobody has the answers.

There is nothing but silence.

Chapter Nine

STARING DOWN AT his hands, Nathan can only see in shades of red and gray.

Demons see the world through different eyes than humans—literally. Humans have the full range of the color spectrum available to them. They see things in bright hues, vibrant greens and blues and reds and yellows. Humans are allowed all the colors of the rainbow. Demonic vision only sees two colors—red, the color of Hell, and black, the color of darkness. White exists too, but the color is a rarity in Nathan's homeland. Even when settled into human form, demons do not get the privilege of seeing the full beauty of color. They see a bit, but colors look faded and washed out, like a watercolor painting left to rot in the summer sun.

The world is not beautiful for demons. Beauty is a luxury they are not allowed.

Nathan flexes his all-too-human hands and watches each joint bend. They are calloused, worn from work and strain. One nail is bleeding—he's been picking at it without realizing. His knuckles on his right hand are scraped. Lines are etched deep into his palms, like cracks in ancient stone.

He didn't lay a hand on anyone. Since he's been on Earth, he brought harm onto a single human. The closest he came was when Tresser attacked him, and even then, he only disabled him.

He did not come here to be a weapon.

"Nate."

The voice startles him out of his reverie. He sits up straight. Tresser is standing in the doorway, hands in his pockets, brows furrowed. His eyes linger on Nathan's hands before shifting back to him, and they both hear the question he does not voice.

"How is everyone?" Nathan asks, in lieu of answers he doesn't have. Tresser sighs, shoulders slumping as if burdened by an invisible weight.

"Well, Lehexe is pissed off. Won't leave the kid—Beck—" He has to visibly correct himself, as if he needs to be reminded that the ones who died were real people. "He won't leave his body. Or the girl's. Hell, even Morgan's. He's acting like they were his responsibility."

They *were*. Beck and Alyssa put their trust in Adam. He did everything to protect them, to shield them against the horrors of what their new lives carried with them. In an instant, all that work was lost. Their trust shattered. Their lives snuffed out.

With a flash of light, a surge of anger, and a demon being forced out of existence.

Just like that.

Five years to the day Nathan came into existence, he was first labeled a monster. Demons can live for millennia; five years, in the lifespan of a single demon, is nothing. Nathan was hardly an infant when people began to fear him for what he could do.

They called him *Interitus*.

Tresser would recognize it as Latin for destruction. For Nathan, the word was a brand upon his skin, a scarlet letter he was forced to bear for his entire life.

Many horrible things lurk in the Ninth Quadrant of Hell; yet somehow, Nathan was made to feel like the worst of them. When he was new, with little control over his own powers, people feared him. They would whisper when he moved past, cringe away, be threatened by his very presence. Their contempt was the cage that barred Nathan in, trapping and isolating him from the rest of the world. Slowly, he realized that he was not like everyone else. He never would be.

Still, he hoped. He hoped and yearned, with all the desperation of a naïve child with nothing to lose, that he would one day find acceptance among his peers.

It was the High Demon Lucius, Duke of the Ninth Quadrant, that shattered these immature fantasies. Lucius practically raised Nathan. The young demon revered him like an icon, more legend than life. When his idol told him that he was more of a weapon than a demon, it struck him like a dagger between the ribs.

"Your power," Lucius said, "is to destroy."

Even then, Nathan knew this wasn't true. It took him many years before he was able to understand what his powers are: not blind devastation, but transmutation. His ability to seize control of demonic energy has gone unparalleled in the history of demonkind. Combined with the capability to direct it, to choose to absorb it into himself or destroy it entirely, Nathan is a weapon. He is revolutionary and deadly. One flash of his temper, and he could destroy an entire demonic army. His abilities are more than unheard of; they are terrifying.

At the time, desperate and afraid of himself, Nathan hadn't known this. His gifts were a curse, and any option seemed better than bearing them for the rest of his life. "What if I don't *want* my powers?" Nathan had asked his mentor

He still remembers the look on Lucius's face; the way the older demon had not softened at all as he leaned forward to place a hand on his shoulder. "There is no way to deny what you are," Lucius told him. "The gifts you are born with are what you are meant to do. They are not who you are meant to be." When he looked down upon him, grim and calm, it struck Nathan at once that these would be the most important words he would ever hear. "Your abilities are a great weapon," his mentor said. "You don't want to be defined by them? Then prove that you are even greater."

Nathan tried. Through Hell and back, he *tried.*

No words before or since have ever struck his heart in exactly the same way. Lucius's creed pierced to the very core of his being. He could never forget it; he could never deny himself the wisdom he was given.

The rest of his life has been spent trying to *make up* for what he can do. He thinks, often, that he has risen above it. He is a fair and judicious person. He has ingrained in himself a level head, patience, and understanding that took years to acquire. He has not risen in the army by the merits of his dangerous ability, but through his own skill and leadership. *This* he has made sure of—he fought to be recognized and promoted on the virtue of his own self. Nathan has worked his way up to become one of the Alliance's most respected Knights and leaders.

Not because of his abilities. Because of *himself.*

(He tells himself this every day, but there are still moments where he cannot push away doubt.)

He did not come to earth to hurt; he came to heal. He did not come to reap destruction, to hear *Interitus* whispered over his shoulder. He came to liberate, not to bring ruin.

Now three people lie dead, another is broken, his Unit is out there without a leader, and Nathan Wentworth is hiding in a psychic's guest room.

This is hardly the behavior of a great man.

"Nate," Tresser says, and drags Nathan's attention back to him again. It is so easy to get lost staring down at his hands; he nearly forgot the human was still here. Tresser stares at him, eyes piercing and almost as dark as a demon's. He crosses the room in a few long strides and settles down on the bed next to Nathan.

"All right. Talk to me now, because you're caught in your head, and that helps nobody. We need to figure this out."

"Tresser—" Nathan starts, and then stops. He takes a deep breath; he sighs; and all the words he wishes would come out jam at the back of his throat, a drain blocked in the middle of a flood. The only thing that comes out is *"Tresser."* His next sigh bears the weight of the world.

When Nathan's gaze drifts back down to his hands, Tresser reaches out and seizes them. "What is it?" he says again, pulling his hands up so Nathan is forced to look at him.

Why doesn't he *know?* It's obvious. It is written plain as day; in Nathan's head, across his face, in the room of death downstairs. "It's my fault."

"That's bullshit," Tresser replies. "It's not anybody's fault. You did the only thing that worked. You can't fault yourself for that." Nathan stares down at his hands, clasped in Tresser's own. The other man heaves a sigh. "And yet..."

"People died," Nathan mutters. Bitterness fills his mouth as the words fall from his lips. "Because of what I did, innocent people lost their lives. That demon was the only thing keeping Matt Morgan alive. Matt Morgan was the only thing keeping the others alive. His death killed them, and I killed him. I *killed him,* Tresser."

When he looks up, there is a smile upon his lips. It is brittle, and tastes like dust, but it is there. "And you know why? I did it because I was angry."

He saw Tresser fly across the room, and suddenly there were no washed out colors or shades of gray. Nathan could only see red—pure, blinding red—and it consumed him.

He lost his temper, and the price was lives. Countless lives, not just the ones upstairs. Who knows how many reanimated people suddenly dropped dead once more? Their blood is on Nathan's hands, and there is no way around it. He does not want to hear Tresser's condolences, his denials, his weak attempts at shifting the blame away. Nathan knows what he's done, and it is the burden he must bear. Wherever he goes, he will always be *Interitus.*

Tresser is silent for a moment. Before he speaks, he sighs. His grip tightens around Nathan's hand, drawing the demon's black eyes to him once more.

"Okay," Tresser says. "It's your fault. So, what are you going to do now?"

Nathan blinks.

"I mean, you've accepted the blame. You've beat yourself up. Now what? Don't tell me you're going to just wallow, because that doesn't sound like you. I was starting to respect you a bit." Tresser's lips quirk up into a smirk, fiercely challenging. Nathan is stunned. "So. Now you have two choices. You can do nothing, or you can do something. You might not be able to make anything right, but those are your options. What are you going to do, Nate?"

Nathan stares at him and takes a breath. His lungs fill up with air instead of sulfur. It is the first clean breath he's taken in hours.

He knows what he has to do, he realizes. He's known it all along.

Slowly, he straightens up. His eyes linger on Tresser as he pulls his hands away. If he had a human heart, it would pound in his chest. As it is, he can only stare and marvel and the incomprehensible, bemusing human in front of him. Tresser makes everything seem so black-and-white; as if he is the one who sees the world in monochrome.

In this moment, it's exactly what Nathan needs.

"Well, when you put it that way," he says, "I guess I'll have to go to Hell."

NATHAN HAS BEEN to Gehenna just once, during the steady ascent of his military career. He remembers it as if it were yesterday.

This was back before the civil war, back when the armies were united, and free travel through the sectors was still encouraged for those who could afford it. Nathan spent his life in Quadrant Nine—the most chaotic of Hell's territories, where terrorism and violence wreaked havoc—and had never ventured out of his corner of the world before. Very few demons ever get to leave their Quadrant and seeing the rest of Hell firsthand; only High Demons are granted the privilege, if you could call it that. There are many parts of Hell Nathan would have been happier to never see.

He remembers Quadrant One, with its polluted landscape and moldy air too thick to breathe; Quadrant

Two, a veritable gulag, where the mass of faceless workers were expected to labor until they dropped; the sleek, technology-driven metal kingdom that was Quadrant Three, mechanical eyes watching your every move. In Quadrant Four, it was almost impossible to see anything at all; Malephor's home city was entirely underground, devoid of all light, the victim of frequent cave-ins and floods. Quadrant Five's has its fire and brimstone, rivers gushing crimson, and earthen pits that opened their fang-toothed maws to swallow you whole. In Quadrant Six, the world was a modern monochromatic Pleasantville, so similar to a human suburbia…save for The Thing That Dwells beneath the streets, keeping all of its residents in line. Monsters lurked behind shadows of skeleton trees in Quadrant Eight, terrorizing the massive winter forest and the small settlements of demons within. Compared to all this, Quadrant Nine—with its bombs and fires, collapsing buildings and broken streets—almost seemed like paradise.

In spite of all the indescribable sights of Hell, it was Quadrant Seven that left the greatest impression on Nathan's mind.

Seven now exists as the beating heart of the Righteous Legion. If he were to step foot into those streets now, it would be suicide; but Nathan remembers. He will never forget the way the residents stared at him as he passed, all seeming to breathe as one entity; or the feeling of omniscient eyes studying his every movement. The sky above was a swirling, blood-filled red, like the heart of a pomegranate. The city itself…was alive. It pulsed beneath his feet, a living entity. When he stumbled over a street curb, his foot dislodged a cobblestone. Viscous black liquid oozed out of the wound, a sickly cocktail of tar, pus, and sulfur.

At the center of Quadrant Seven, of course, was Hell's pride and joy: The Pits of Gehenna.

Even by the standards of Hell itself, Gehenna was a nightmare. Legends were told about the indomitable fortress and the chasm that it guarded. No one came out of the Pits; those who looked inside would never be the same. So the legend goes, at least; Nathan is living proof to refute those claims. He *did* go into Gehenna, and he returned.

Was he the same afterwards? Well, that's a different question.

If everything about Quadrant Seven felt alive, Gehenna was dead. It did not pulse with life or energy; it remained a mole on the chest of the Quadrant. Yet somehow that mole managed to rest right over Quadrant Seven's heart.

The Pits were something incomprehensible; something more than alive. They were ancient; older than demons, older than humanity. They should not have existed, but they *did*. Beneath Gehenna's unassuming cover, the Pits swallowed up everything and everyone.

Nathan only saw a glimpse of the Pits. The memory will never leave him.

Somehow, he has to lead his men straight into enemy territory. Straight into Gehenna. Straight into the Pits.

It should not be possible.

Once he begins organizing his men, however, Nathan finds his that he hadn't counted on a few crucial variables. For one, the men of Unit X's loyalty to him; for another, Adam Lehexe and Cassandra Carlyle's very human magic.

"You demons can't get in there on your own?" Adam demands, bent double over a sheet of paper spread out on the table. "Then leave it to us."

His hand is possessed by a mind of its own. It flies across the paper, sketching out spells and sigils in spidery print. He does not look up at the room around him, nor does he hesitate. Adam is a deep well of magical information, brimming over onto the page. Cassandra stands at his side, muttering to him. Every so often, she points out inconsistencies in his scribbles, and he writes over it. They are both locked in intense focus. Their plan looks incomprehensible to Nathan; then again, he knows very little about witchcraft.

"Humans can't breach the barriers of Hell," Malephor protests, sounding affronted. Cassandra tears her eyes from the paper just long enough to smirk.

"Normal humans, no. Yet it's been done before. Someone had to tear that gap in the barrier in the first place, right? That's where all this started. So if someone could open the barrier between worlds once, unintentionally..." Her eyes gleam. "Who's to say it can't be done on purpose?"

If anyone can do it, it's Adam Lehexe. Tresser explained to him earlier that the Lehexe family was one of the most powerful magical families in Louisiana, maybe even the whole country. Adam has generations of magical blood in his veins.

What's more, he's *angry*. Adam's lost enough to this disaster; he's suffered his own war casualties. He's got as much invested in this as Nathan and is so set on helping that it's a little frightening.

Only a fool dares to cross a pissed-off witch. Nathan is no fool.

So, the witches lay out a plan; and by the end of two hours, they've got it.

"We focus all our energies on Gehenna and punch a hole right through the barrier. It'll create a two-way door—you can all get in, while the demons there can get out."

"It's too risky," Tresser declares immediately. "You'd be letting all of those hell-beasts loose on the town. That's just what they want."

Cassandra shakes her head. "Not if I reverse my wards. Right now, this place is like a bubble—the wards keep any demon who I haven't let in personally out. If I could turn that around, they would all be trapped inside the bubble with no way to escape to the town at large."

"Trapped," Tresser says slowly, "inside your house?"

Cassandra presses her lips into a thin line.

"We can't do it," says Malephor. "It's too risky."

"Which is why someone needs to stay behind," Nathan interjects. All eyes turn to him; he straightens up under the scrutiny. If the plan were perfect, then no demons would escape into the human world at all. If the plan were perfect, they would have more time to plan, more soldiers to execute it. They would have more options and less risk.

No plans are perfect. Adam and Cassandra's idea is the best one they've got.

"Sergeant Malephor, your mission is to guard the barrier. Any Grey that comes through is an enemy. You neutralize them."

Malephor stares at him for a long moment, face unreadable. Were Nathan not growing attuned to the subtle inflections of Malephor, he would wonder if she understood him. "That's a combat position, sir," she finally says, as if to verify his words. He nods.

"I am aware."

A deep satisfaction settles over Malephor's face. "I will defend the human world against all intrusions," she declares.

Once they've got a way in, the rest of the uncertainties begin to melt away. Planning and technicalities are things that make sense to Nathan. These are things he can anticipate and control, to the benefit of his men. Plans can be worked out easily.

It helps that he has Tresser on his side. Tresser proves himself to be a tactical genius. Once he's gotten a quick layout of whatever intelligence Nathan has of the Fortress of Gehenna (which isn't much but will have to be enough), he's able to pinpoint the most likely places for armed guards to be positioned, the obvious points of attack, and the best way to infiltrate without being noticed until it's too late. Tresser's brain is sharp as a needle, and he's quick on his feet; he comes up with a solution to a problem as soon as Nathan can think one up. It isn't long before they have a workable strategy.

They storm Gehenna, rescue the human prisoners, and destroy as much of the stronghold as they can. If possible, they even get out alive.

By late in the evening, Nathan has met with his sergeants and sent them out to prepare their squads. Abraxas looks dubious but agrees to the plan; Nemphis is loyal as ever; Valac is ready for anything.

It is Nathan's human allies who surprise him the most. While he counted on loyalty from his men, he never thought that the humans would want to be part of the plan.

"Of course we're coming!" declares Henry, who's been hanging off of Nathan's every word like a starving man desperate for crumbs of food. Each mention of the prison sets him alight. When Nathan explains their plans to free the captives, he is practically thrumming with pent-up adrenaline. "If the plan is to blast the cells open and save everybody, you need all the manpower you can get!"

"Humans can't survive for long in hell," Nathan protests. There's no way he's leading Henry into hell. Not only is he a mortal, but he's also untrained and inexperienced in combat. Nathan saw Henry flounder in the middle of the office battle. Against a fortress of demons, he'd be powerless. He's too much of a risk.

Henry looks determined; he is dead-set on this. His hands are clenched into fists at his side, as if he can barely contain himself, and there is a desperation in his face that Nathan has never seen before. "Lucy and the others are being kept alive," he insists, fast and breathless. "So you have a group of people outside of your fighting group, people who are focused on rescuing the prisoners. I'll get her. All I'm talking is five minutes. In and out, just like that. *Take me with you.*"

Nathan can't do that. "I'm sorry."

"You don't get to be *sorry,*" Henry spits. He recoils as if Nathan has just struck him; then, he forces himself to take a deep breath. When he speaks again, his words are calmer but no less resolute. "I'm *going* to bring Lucy home. If I've got to go to hell and back to do it, I will. Take me, Nate. I'm your best shot. I'll get her out."

They don't *know* how heavily guarded Gehenna will be. Henry might have a point. If the rest of the unit seizes the prison while a few people infiltrate the cells to get the prisoners out...

It might be their best shot.

Tresser clears his throat, startling Nathan. When he turns, he finds Tresser's sharp gaze trained on him. Nathan suddenly feels like he's been shot in the chest. He recognizes the look in Tresser's eyes, in the determined quirk to his lips, and knows what he is about to say before the words pass his lips.

"He means *we* will. We'll kick every prisoner out of there, so you can swoop in and blow that place to...well, you get the idea."

"Tresser, no."

Tresser grins at him. "Come on, I can't miss my chance to go to Hell. I'll actually be doing what my father tells me for once! And *y'know,* it's a once in a lifetime vacation spot."

"You could get hurt."

"So could you." Tresser's words are unfazed, almost amused. Just as quickly, they turn serious. "I'm going, Nate."

Nathan says nothing. There is nothing he can say that will talk Tresser out of itand nothing Tresser can say that will convince him not to be afraid. The thought of losing this man, this *friend,* the first human he has ever known; who he learns about and respects more with each passing minute, who is so good at leaving him speechless... He could not stand to lose David Tresser.

The thought makes him feel young, he realizes. Young and vulnerable, uncertain in a way he hasn't felt in centuries. It's a shock to his system. He's seen more in his lifetime than a human could ever imagine; and still, he is afraid.

Afraid of leading his company to their deaths. Afraid of losing all he's cared about—his career, his life, and this strange human who is the first friend he's ever had. Afraid that this is how he will be remembered. Legacies don't matter to him, they really don't—but he doesn't want to be immortalized as *Interitus*.

He is afraid that he will get David Tresser killed.

Tresser looks at him, solemn and sober, determined and unguarded. Nathan has never seen him this way before. It startles him. In a split second, he realizes that Tresser *understands*.

"I trust you," Tresser says.

I trust you.

They are the simplest words in the world, but they mean something coming from Tresser's lips. They mean the same thing to two very different men. Tresser is spun from lies and deceptions, passion and fear, layered beneath a smooth, sardonic veneer. Nathan is molded from clay and carved in stone, as honest as the earth that does not belong to him. In this way, he is a bigger fraud than Tresser.

They hear these words exactly the same way.

I trust you.

It means everything all at once, and when Nathan takes a deep breath, he finds that he can breathe.

"We leave bright and early tomorrow," he tells Henry and Tresser. "Be ready."

By the time the sergeants depart, the plan is in place. Company X will assemble at sunrise. They will spend one more night cleansing the last of the Greys from Earth. Tomorrow, they will storm Gehenna.

In the meantime, all that's left to do is wait.

NATHAN DOESN'T SLEEP that night. This isn't a big deal; technically, Nathan does not have to sleep at all.

Human circadian rhythms are an enigma to him, so he's not sure how a sleep schedule even works, but he's pretty sure Tresser should not be wide awake past midnight as well.

"You need sleep," he says, slipping the cellphone from Tresser's hands in one deft motion. The man does not reach for it. He just blinks, as if he can't believe Nathan really has the *audacity*.

Tresser recovers after a moment. "I do not. Gimme." He reaches for the phone, but Nathan sets it down on the dresser, out of his reach. Tresser is too lazy to sit up and reach for it. Or maybe he's just as tired as he looks.

"Lack of sleep makes for an incompetent soldier," Nathan tells him (which he supposes is true, for humans). "I want you at your best out there. As good as you were in the office today."

Tresser's lips curve in a molasses-slow smirk. "You think that was my best? You ain't seen nothing yet, Nate."

"I look forward to it, then." Nathan slides off of his end of the twin bed and nods for Tresser to take over. He won't sleep tonight, so Tresser may as well make use of the extra space. Only when Tresser frowns at him, unimpressed, does Nathan realize he might not see it the same way.

"And what about you?"

"I've got too much to think about."

"Well, think about it over here." Tresser pats the side of the bed again. Nathan sighs. It's funny how he's never had a problem arguing with others before, but Tresser seems to steal all his protests before he can even voice them.

"I didn't think," he says as he slips back under the bed's neon-checkered comforter, "that you enjoyed sharing the bed with me last night."

"Humans kick in their sleep, Nate. That's involuntary. Sorry if I bruised you."

"It wasn't that." Nathan frowns as he recalls Tresser's face from the curious moments spent watching him the night before. The way his brows had furrowed, teeth bared and lips twisting, as if he were in the throes of some fierce argument. The way he thrashed. The occasional whimpers. Whatever sleep had hold of Tresser last night, it was certainly not a restful one. "You seemed upset."

Tresser is silent for a long moment. Thoughtful green eyes stare up at the cracked ceiling. He is not offended by the question, simply pensive.

"Do you know what a dream is, Nate?" he asks after a moment.

"Dreams are the projections of the unconscious mind humans experience when they sleep." He rolls his eyes. "I'm a demon, not an alien."

"What about a nightmare?"

"Bad dreams," Nathan says automatically. Then: "Oh."

"Oh," affirms Tresser. When he turns his head towards Nathan, a faint smile ghosts his lips. "I don't have many good ones."

Nathan has no idea what to say. *I'm sorry* seems callous. *That's all right* seems dismissive. *I understand* would be a lie.

"Why?" he asks instead.

To his credit, Tresser doesn't look fazed. He just lets out a huff that isn't really a laugh, leaning back against his pillow. When he tucks a hand behind his head, his elbow brushes Nathan's shoulder.

"Imagine this: you're five years old, and you believe in monsters. Every little kid is afraid of monsters, right?

Except for you, it's different, because you know the monsters are real. Every shadow in the closet, every bump under your bed, every weird sound outside your window...there's not any question whether it might be a monster, because you know it could. Hell, it probably is. All the things you've ever been afraid of are real. They shouldn't be, but they are. And of all the families in the world, *yours* is the one who gets the privilege of keeping all those shouldn't-be's from destroying the world."

He takes a deep breath and blows it out towards the ceiling. "You know what my father used to tell me? He'd always say I had nothing to be afraid of...because I'm a human being. And 'humans are the biggest monsters of them all'. To a five-year-old kid."

He falls silent and turns away again. Nathan can't see his face, but Tresser's word sear into his mind like a red-hotiron brand.

As a child, Tresser used to be afraid of the very things he's devoted his life to fighting. Tresser never got the chance to be a child; nor was he ever able to grow up. In many ways, David Tresser is still a scared little boy hiding beneath his covers from shadowy arms that stretch out of his bedroom closet.

Tomorrow, Tresser is going straight into the den of monsters; and Nathan is leading him there. If something goes wrong, Tresser's blood will be on Nathan's hands.

It all seems wrong. So wrong that, for a second, Nathan is overwhelmed by it. Tresser deserved a better life, the sort Nathan never got the chance to live. Tresser deserves more than this. He does not deserve to die on a vendetta mission to Hell.

"I'm one of those monsters," Nathan says quietly. "You know that, right?"

Tresser sits up. For a moment, all he does is stare at Nathan. His eyes are hard, his face unreadable; there is no trace of sympathy, of fear, of shame. Tresser is a blank slate. A storm of emotion swirls beneath the stolid veneer of his face, but Nathan cannot breach that. He doesn't try. It isn't his place to take what Tresser won't give.

"Yeah. I know," Tresser finally says—and then he does something that Nathan never expected.

He swoops in and kisses him. It is only for a handful of seconds, but those seconds seem to drag on for centuries. Nathan is hit with the full force of everything— from the dryness of Tresser's lips, the taste of mint and cigarettes, the calloused hand holding the back of his head steady—all at once. If he had any need to breathe, his breath would have been stolen. His heart would have stopped beating. As it is, he can only remain still for the precious seconds that the kiss drags on...until the last, when he remembers to kiss back.

When they pull away, they are only inches from each other. Tresser's eyes are dark pools of incomprehensible emotion, inches away from Nathan's face. Nathan can only stare into them, hazy and exhilarated at the same time.

Tresser smirks. "Except I'm not scared of monsters anymore."

Nathan takes a deep breath and presses his hand against the muscled plane of Tresser's chest. He is deliciously solid against him, real in all the ways that count. There is no way to doubt what just happened. In this moment, with the taste of Tresser still burning on his lips, tomorrow seems like nothing more than a fantasy.

It is present, but unreal. Something that will happen, but not the only thing that matters.

Slowly, Nathan exhales a breath against Tresser's mouth.

"You saved my life today," he mutters. "Are you willing to have my back one last time?"

Tresser's head tilts. "Who says it has to be the last? That was a promise, Nate. A just-in-case."

"Just in case of what?" Nathan asks, smirking.

"Just in case," replies Tresser, "we make it through tomorrow. That will be the beginning—not the end."

A beginning. Nathan can live with a beginning. If, of course, they live at all.

He nods and slowly pushes Tresser away. All of a sudden, the sunrise doesn't seem nearly as foreboding.

Chapter Ten

THE SUN RISES.

By dawn, Cassandra's parlor is illuminated by a veil of candlelight. The incense in the air is so cloying that it's almost impossible to take a breath. Everything is less real, now. The flames flickering off the walls do not just add a surreal feeling to the proceedings but shatter the boundary between fantasy and reality completely.

Standing in the center of the room, Tresser's head swims like he's coming off a three-day bender. Across from him, Nathan is cool and solemn, scowl carved deep into his fine-boned face.

Somehow, this seems fitting. The last glimpse of this world he will get before descending to the next is of Nathan Wentworth, who doesn't even belong in this world to begin with.

"You kissed me last night," Tresser says, too low for anyone but Nathan to hear. "Do you regret it?"

Nathan doesn't blink. "Absolutely not. Do you?"

"No," he answers, smirking. "So, don't die today, okay?"

The smallest of smiles tugs at Nathan's lips. "Same to you."

"I'll do my best."

There is a sputter of candle flame as Cassandra crosses the room. She holds a glistening golden rod, engraved with trails of copper and crimson. When she lifts it up, it captures all the light in the room.

"Stand in the circle, everyone," Adam announces. The assembled travelers obligingly move into the center of the circle that has been etched on the floor. It's a bit small to accommodate the entirety of Unit X—about twenty guys in all. Tresser stands on the edge of the circle next to Henry, who is practically vibrating with nervous energy.

Tresser can relate. There is no need to ask if everyone is ready. They are all *more* than ready. There is no hesitation among the mass of people, human and demon alike. It feels like magma is pulsing through Tresser's veins; his mounting adrenaline makes it nearly impossible to keep still. As soon as his feet touch the ground in Hell, he's going to take off running.

Cassandra and Adam stand at separate points of the circle, arms out at their sides. Tresser is close enough to Adam to see his eyes close, to notice the shudder of breath that leaves him, and the way he is utterly still afterwards. For a long moment, silence hangs over the room, choking the air from *everyone's* lungs. When Tresser shifts, his body feels heavy, as if he is drowning in molasses.

Cassandra begins to chant, her voice a low melody:
"The light of worlds descends upon
the veil that is now yet to close.
Release the chains that bind us here
and let the barriers unfurl."
"Shatter the divide," Adam invokes. *"Ad ignotis locos."*

The shadows dance along the walls, hissing sweet promises in Tresser's ears. He feels their hands caress him, electrifying his limbs. He feels stripped bare. His heart is rising out of his body, taking his soul with it. There is no air left to breathe.

"Destroy the seals," Adam invokes. "Break the barrier."

Two pairs of hands come together with a resounding *crash*, and the tension is shattered. In the aftermath of the clap, Tresser blinks through his daze, searching the room for any sign of what was meant to happen. There's nothing. Cassandra's parlor is the same as ever; the shadows have faded once again.

"Wait," Cassandra says. "It's coming."

That's all she gets the chance to say. In the next second, a great rumble seems to rise from the core of the earth. The entire house rattles; dishes rap at their cabinet confinements, the grandfather clock against the wall tips over and smashes, pictures quake against the walls. Tresser is almost thrown off his feet. He grabs on to Henry for balance, and the two hold each other up against the forces of gravity.

Cassandra grips the wall with hands to steady herself. She does not see the destruction being reaped throughout her house. Her gaze is trained only on the space above the circle, above all of their heads. The whites of her eyes stand out in her drawn, pale face.

Tresser looks up as well, and the breath is sucked from his lungs.

There is a gap in the world. It cuts above his head like a jagged scar, stretching out to consume the entire circle. The gap writhes and pulses with energy, electricity flashing in white-violet bursts. Something incomprehensible swirls within its depths, older, *deeper*, than anything Tresser has ever seen.

He is suddenly certain that the existence of this opening which should not be is *wrong*. It steals his breath, snatches the heart from his chest. It terrifies him.

This is it, he realizes, feeling Henry's hand tighten around his arm. *To Hell and back again...hopefully.*

He takes one step forward. In an instant, everything he's ever known vanishes.

When Tresser opens his eyes, a red sky churns above his head.

ENTERING HELL AGAIN feels like a bubble bursting.

Nathan never registered the tension that has been strung throughout his body, the pressure buried deep within his bones, until he sets foot in his world once again. At once, it feels like a coil snapping. It's as if he's been underwater and finally surfaced for air. This is home; this is the world he belongs in, the air he is supposed to breathe.

Of course, he isn't home, not really. Quadrant Seven is a vastly different world from Nathan's homeland. Here, smog doesn't choke the air, and the distant, omnipresent wail of sirens is absent. Quadrant Nine is nothing like this place, this living, breathing city, but it is still Hell, and it is enough. He is assaulted with everything; every sense and smell, every inch of the atmosphere. It reminds him of home. For the first second he is left breathless.

Then a bolt of lightning shoots past his head, and everything rushes back to him at once. Nathan knows exactly where he is and what he's supposed to be doing.

They've materialized in the very heart of enemy territory. Quadrant Seven heaves a breath beneath their feet. The Fortress of Gehenna towers in front of them, a massive omnibus of steel and brick. From the outside, it looks impenetrable.

Nathan knows better.

His eyes land on the demon guard atop the lowest walls of the prison, just beginning to get their bearings and shoot the intruders. There are three guards, and at twenty-three intruders. In the time it takes the Greys to process that their base has been infiltrated, Unit X is already surging forward to attack.

A scythe slams into the head of a Grey just feet in front of Nathan. To his left, Valac attacks with the force of one who has never known mercy. To his right, Charus launches himself into the final of Grey, sword swinging. Oily blood spatters the stone beneath their feet.

Just like that, Gehenna has been breached.

"Seriously?" demands Henry. "That should not have been so easy."

The impenetrable fortress derives much of its notoriety from reputation alone. No prisoner ever comes out of Gehenna; so why would anyone want to break in?

Unit X charges over the lower wall, and from there it's a clear shot straight into the prison. Nathan counts his men as they file past, checking off each one in his head. Maggus, Janec, Abraxas, Charrus, Chorso...they are all here. All alive. Inside Gehenna.

Henry and Tresser are last, following Nathan's lead inside the prison walls. The humans cannot have expected the sheer quality of darkness they are confronted with. In Hell, darkness is not simply the absence of light. It is dense, tangible emptiness, as capable of smothering as it is of concealing. Darkness is alive in Hell, and especially in Quadrant Seven.

Nathan jerks to a stop, his Unit charging forward, when Tresser catches him. "Where are the humans being held, then? The actual Pits?"

Nathan shakes his head. As long as they're useful to them, the Legion would never throw their prisoners into the Pits. The Pits are eternal; they consume all that is and ever was. There is no returning from the Pits.

He flashes back to his tour of the place so many years ago and comes up with a quick answer. "No. There are lines of cells along the way down. The pathway winds, and the turns are steep; eventually it opens out into the Pit itself. If there are prisoners being held anywhere, it would be there."

"That's where we go, then," says Henry.

Tresser makes to pull away, but Nathan holds him fast. "Be careful," he orders, too focused on his role as Unit leader to remember to be anything else. "There may be things other than kidnapped humans in those cells. Don't let out what you don't recognize. As soon as you have the prisoners, call Cassandra to pull you out of there. And whatever you do—" His hand tightens around Tresser's upper arm. "Once the cells stop, don't follow the path any further. There's no coming back from the Pits."

He can just see Tresser's eyes studying him in the near-blackness, sharp and concentrated. When he nods, Nathan squeezes him again.

"You have your comm links?"

Tresser hums, tapping the device attached to his ear (to keep them connected while inside the prison, and to their allies above). Henry does the same. Nathan checks his last, feeling the reassuring weight of it against his neck. "Either of you run into trouble, you call me."

"Yes, sir," Henry answers. Tresser says nothing.

Ahead of them, howls begin to echo throughout the cavernous prison halls. Nathan's only reassurance is that he recognized them as Grey screams.

He can't dwell here any longer; he has to fight alongside his men. They need him now.

"All right." He claps both men on the shoulders, a distinctly human gesture. "Follow the next side pathway you find. They all lead to the same place. If you run into any trouble—"

"Take 'em out," Tresser confirms. "I've killed demons before."

No, he hasn't, but Nathan doesn't tell him that. Exorcizing and killing a demon are two very different things, but there is no time to explain now. There's no time for talking, for well wishes, for goodbyes. They are out of time altogether.

As if reading his thoughts, in that peculiar way Tresser always seems to have, he feels a squeeze on his hand. It is a wordless gesture, but it speaks more than Tresser could ever say. I trust you. Trust me too, huh?

Nathan has no choice.

"All right," he says, taking a step away. "Good luck."

He rushes off to join his Unit and does not glance back at the men he's leaving behind. There is no time for fear.

Now, all he can do is fight.

AS SOON AS the earth ceases to quake, Malephor is ready for battle. She stands poised at the edge of the circle, clawed hands braced at her sides, tense and coiled like a viper seconds from pouncing. When Cassandra looks at her, she remembers how to breathe again. For just a moment, the sight of the portal to hell had driven all the breath from her lungs.

"How many will come?" Adam shouts over the roar of the portal.

"No way of knowing. Could be five. Could be five hundred."

The Demon-Human barrier has been breached once again. Now they are the only thing that stands between a Legion of bloodthirsty demons and the rest of the human world.

Cassandra's legs feel weak, but she forces herself to stand. She can do this. If this was what she was born for all along, she *will* do this.

A buzz of static sounds in her ear; over the poor connection, she hears the faint trill of a voice. "Cassie, you read me?"

"Gotcha, Henry," she answers over. If Henry is speaking to them, that means they made it into the fortress alive. Now, all Cassandra has to do on her end is pull them out—and, you know, not die, but that's a given.

The portal ripples; the house shudders again. She curses as one of her framed pictures slides off the wall and crashes to the floor. A pulse of energy strong enough to knock her off balance rolls from the portal, and Cassandra's back hits the wall behind her once more.

The portal is alive, she realizes. It is as much of a sentient thing as anyone else in this room.

Dead things have never scared Cassandra; it's the living that truly frightens her.

A sudden shout from Malephor draws her focus to her, but it is torn away just as quickly when something tumbles out of the portal. It hits the ground hard, snarling and screeching; Cassandra can barely recognize it as a mangy black dog before it launches itself straight at Malephor.

There is no second of hesitation. Malephor slashes her claws straight through it, severing it into pieces, and the demon drops.

He is just the beginning, though. The next second, a dozen great bats, as wide as Cassandra's arms, flow out of the portal. The nearest one does not take a second to orient itself; it flies straight at Cassandra's head.

Screeches fill the air, and claws lash at her vulnerable eyes. She screeches, throwing up her hands to protect herself. Its claws bite into her vulnerable flesh.

The battle has entered the human world, in the very worst way.

THERE ARE MANY ways to kill a human, but very few methods of actually killing a demon. Demons are eternal. They live forever in the space between breaths, in the shadows behind open doorways, beneath the cracks in walls, and the whispers in silence. Demons do not die. They simply cease to exist.

Nathan's method of snuffing out a demon entirely is the crudest, as well as the most effective. The only way to compare it, he imagines, would be a human being vaporized—to go from *something* to *nothing* in an instant. Nathan's brand of destruction leaves not an echo behind.

There are demons powerful enough to fight others with their bare hands; and weapons that can be used in the most brutal of ways, to sever a demon's body clean through. These weapons are enchanted to be violent, to be devastating. If used right, they can kill. These are the average demon's weapons of warfare, and Nathan is no less vulnerable to them than any other.

A sword decapitates a demon next to him, spattering him with hot blood. Nathan grits his teeth and pushes forward. His own shield guards him from any well-aimed attacks. He leads the charge with his men behind him, pushing forward into the fortress and cutting down any Grey who stands in their way.

Further. *Further.* They have to keep going, have to keep attacking. They have to draw all the fire, so that Tresser and Henry can—

"We're in, Nate," Tresser's voice chimes in his ear. Nathan grunts as he takes the head off of a demon who dares to get too close. *"Then again, you sound like you're doing your own thing. Take your time."*

"Appreciated," Nathan mutters in reply, ducking a swing towards his throat. Tresser had assured him that their communication devices would stay on during the fight, but if he takes a blow to the head, Nathan isn't sure how well the little Bluetooth will hold out. Tresser Corps technology is designed to survive anything, but interdimensional travel and a battle on top of that might be pushing it.

Nathan thrusts his weapon again, catching a Grey in the chest. As that enemy falls, he is faced with two more coming up behind him. Raising his shield high, Nathan blocks an attack to his side and lunges forward, catching one of the Greys in the neck. He goes down gurgling, while the other is incensed by the attack on his friend. He pushes against Nathan's shield, and in a well-timed moment of surprise manages to cast it aside. A mace soars towards Nathan's head. He just manages to duck, lunging forward to catch the Grey in the stomach. Bowled over, the Grey teeters and falls. Nathan thrusts his sword down without looking, and the enemy does not move again.

"Knight Naberos!" Charus's voice rings out above the din. He cleaves another demon before nodding in Nathan's direction. Their battle has attracted most of the manpower of the fortress—meaning the cells must currently be unguarded.

"We're on the pathway now," Tresser says, a second before another sword swings in a round arc towards Nathan's head. He blocks the blow but is distracted by taking him down. He hears nothing more over Tresser's end of the line until a sudden burst of static takes him by surprise.

When Tresser speaks again, his voice comes in much clearer. *"Can hardly see. Did you have a clue flashlights don't work down here? A heads up would have been nice."*

Nathan can't suppress the grim smile that creeps its way across the face. He ducks another blow to the side. "You'll survive, Tresser."

"Here's hoping," Tresser chimes back. After that, Nathan can hear muffled conversation between the two humans, but he's too distracted by the battle raging on around him. Unit X is holding its own; Nathan doesn't think they've lost any men, but they're putting a great dent in the Grey reserves. They function in sync with one another, a well-oiled fighting machine. The knowledge that he is commanding an elite force of the Alliance army floods back to Nathan in full force. He couldn't be happier to be part of such a well-trained unit.

On one side of him, Appolis has taken a high vantage point and is firing off arrow after arrow with lethal accuracy. On his other side, Charus and Chorso fight back to back, a blinding hurricane of blades hitting each target with ease. Passien is quick and furious, darting through his targets too quickly for them to realize it before they're already slumping to the ground, blood bubbling from their gaping throats. Maral is surrounded by a haze of black smoke, forming dizzying illusions around him as he moves through the enemy fighters, stabbing each one through as they're distracted. Valac is a powerhouse all of his own, cutting down anyone who gets in his way.

These are *his men,* and they did not come here to be defeated.

Nathan parries a blow by another High Demon, who then proceeds to lash out with a smoky claw. He catches Nathan across the side. He doubles over with a yell as blood spills from the newly formed gash, but he doesn't give the other demon the chance to do him in. Instead he charges forwards, headbutting him in the chest, and when he reels back, Nathan severs the black claw from the rest of his body. The rest of him is soon to follow. Nathan feels a rush of twisted satisfaction as the body drops to the ground.

(War is not pretty, but it is all he has known. If it ever horrified him, that ceased long ago.)

"Oh god," he suddenly hears over his comm, and for just a second, he freezes. He has never heard that tone in Tresser's voice before—utterly disarmed, halfway between astonishment and horror. His mind is an immediate rush of possibilities. Have they run straight into the enemy? Are they being overrun? Are they too late, and found the prisoners dead?

"Nate," Tresser says, and takes a shaky breath. *"Jesus, Nate, this—this is insane."*

"Tresser, what is it?"

"I—" Tresser says, but his voice dies. Nathan's heart plummets when he cuts himself off with a ragged gasp.

What the hell did they find?

CAGES. EVERYWHERE TRESSER looks, there are cages.

The cells weren't that bad at first. Iron bars stretched across crevasses gauged deep into the wall. The cells higher up in the fortress were tight and cramped, half-concealed by darkness. They would be easy to rush right past, were someone not searching for them. Most of them were empty, devoid of all life; but the ones that were not were unmistakable.

The stench of rot hung heavy in the air, hardly leaving room for the prisoners to breathe. They pressed against the bars because they had nowhere else to go, hissing and snapping whenever someone rushed by. Tresser doesn't count on them recognizing that the strangers who passed them do not belong. For the most part, the prisoners looked delirious. They wouldn't be able to tell friend from foe anyway.

The further they got from Nathan and the others, however, the more obvious it became that this was Hell's most infamous prison. The landscape changed. The cells were emptier, darker. Prisoners were few and far between. Finally, it seemed as if they had run out of cells entirely.

Tresser and Henry kept walking.

And, sure enough, there were more prisoners waiting for them. The very ones they've been searching for.

"Oh god," Henry gags, doubling forward. "Jesus—*Jesus*."

Jesus isn't here right now; this is no place for God, for faith, for civilization. This is Hell at its worst. Tresser reels.

"I—" he starts but chokes on his own words. There is no way to describe what he is seeing. He is incapable of putting the horror into words.

The familiar form of Lucy Dorsett must have been pretty once; now, she is nothing. The emaciated shell of her body hangs from the wall, suspended by chains that keep her arms pinned high above her head. Her feet dangle just over the ground. A mess of blonde curls, greasy and matted with dirt, curtain her bowed head. In spite of all this, there's no mistaking the woman who beamed so proudly from Henry's many pictures. They've found who they're looking for.

"Lucy—oh god, Lucy!" Henry rushes fowards, body slamming against the cell bars. "What the hell are they doing to her, Tresser?"

Tresser doesn't know. His gaze is trained not on Lucy's battered frame or bowed head, but on the lazy streams of blood that seem to drip from every part of her. Dark rivulets run down her arms; her legs; her neck. Narrow, precise slashes draw the blood out; it drips to the floor, only to vanish into what looks like a large drain. The crimson stands out all the more against Lucy's papery-white skin.

Tresser's head reels. His stomach lurches. The horror around him does not evaporate, like the phantom mirages of nightmares, but he wishes, prays it would.

A sudden whimper draws his attention to the side, and a gasp catches in his throat. Where the cells from earlier were sparsely occupied, the ones surrounding him now are full. All of them contain a battered figure strapped to the wall, blood slowly draining from their extremities. Seven cells; seven prisoners.

This is who we came here for, he realizes with a sickening jolt.

"Tresser!" Nathan's voice slices through the din of horror his thoughts have become. *"Tell me what's happening there!"*

There's no good way to describe it. There's no good way to even try, but the horror spills past Tresser's lips anyways. "They're keeping these people locked up in here," he gasps, "like cattle. They're chained to the walls—god, and the floors...what *are* those things?" Tresser is quiet for a moment, able to hear nothing but the raspy sound of his own breathing. Finally he manages a strained, trembling, "What the fuck?"

"Tresser!" Nathan sounds like he's in the middle of chaos of his own. A grunt comes from his end of the line, and Tresser flinches.

"They're taking their blood, Nate! They're draining it! What the hell do they need it for?"

He knows the significance of blood, after all, in both lore and magic. Blood is *life*—it holds an energy revered throughout every world. To demons, however, human blood holds a special significance. It represents something they can never quite obtain: control over humanity. The Greys could be using the blood of psychics and witches, not quite human and not quite magical, for *any* number of things...

But his mind suddenly flashes back to Beck Murray, youthful and vibrant despite being dead for half a year. He thinks of Beck. and all the other people popping out of their graves, and Tresser *knows*.

In an awful way, it's brilliant. To create their own weapons, they reanimated deceased humans using energy that they stole from ones already living. The reanimated humans became open doors for demons to pass through, while the humans they stole...

"Tresser, are they alive?"

Henry slams his entire body against the bars, bellowing his girlfriend's name. Miles away, trapped in her prison, Lucy doesn't even stir. Tresser takes a sharp inhale over the comm system.

"I think so," he pants. "Hell, I'm not sure. All six of them are here. Henry's found Lucy."

Nathan exhales a sigh of relief, but that's all he has time for before the sound of another attack pulls him away from the conversation. Tresser hears the clash of metal against metal, winces when Nathan grunts, and holds his breath until his demon is back on the line.

"Go!" Nathan orders into the comm. *"Take them and get out of there!"*

"HENRY'S BUSY PICKING the locks, hang on—we can only open one at a time," Tresser mutters, voice tight. *"We have to—yeah, Lucy first—they're all in bad shape, Nate. We've got to hurry...how are you holding out?"*

Abraxas drives his sword into the back of the head of the demon Nathan is struggling with, splashing them both with blood. "You know," Nathan says, "doing fine."

"Okay. Great. We're moving fast." There's another blur of static on Tresser's end of the line, and by that point Nathan has to stop paying attention. A new influx of soldiers floods the corridor. Just when Unit X had been turning the tide of the battle, they find themselves outnumbered again, even worse than before.

After that, there is no time for chatter. Nathan can hear Tresser and Henry over the other end of the line going back and forth for prisoners, but he cannot keep up with them. He throws himself into battle with a single-minded focus, knowing that every breath must be spent on leading his men to victory.

He takes lashes to the side, small injuries, scratches and stabs; each time, he pushes forward. He is a High Demon; he knows how to fight, and he knows how to be battered. Every enemy that comes at him finds themselves cut down. Even when his muscles begin to burn and his chest feels tight, Nathan forces himself to fight on. For Unit X; for earth; for Henry, and Lucy, and all the prisoners who couldn't fight for themselves. For Tresser.

He will *not* lead them all to ruin.

More and more enemies pour in from all sides. Maggus is fighting ferociously, Abraxas is plowing forward like a tank, but there is no getting over the sheer numbers. Unit X is beginning to show the first signs of faltering. They're getting slower, less coordinated, their limbs heavier and their minds exhausted.

They can't give up here. Nathan hollers to his men, urging them on, and they continue to fight with all they've got.

"This one?" he hears faintly over the comm. *"We let them all out?"*

"They're all prisoners," Tresser's voice retorts. He hisses a curse under his breath. "Come on, Henry!"

"I'm trying—"

A click of metal. A screech. Nathan drives his sword through an enemy's chest and does not give himself time to wonder, to think. They need to fight.

They are fighting. Unit X isn't going to give up, even if it's down to the last man—and Nathan refuses to let it come to that.

They've got to fight on.

HE REALIZES THEY'VE made a horrible mistake the second the chains fall away from the last prisoner's wrists, and he lifts his head all on his own.

It could mean anything. He hasn't been here as long as the others, maybe. He hasn't been trapped as long, been drained of quite so much life. But the rivulets of blood coursing down his bare skin quickly reverse direction, retreating back up instead of down, and Tresser realizes.

The prisoner lifts his head and twitches it to the side. His eyes are a bright, blazing red.

Henry lets out a shout, reeling back from the open cell door. Tresser moves to close it, but it's too late; it is far too late. In a single bound, the creature who is *definitely not human* swoops out of the cell.

An unholy screech pierces the air. It echoes in the core of Tresser's soul. He drops to the ground, both hands clamped over his ears as wave after wave of pain pulses through his head. When he pulls his hands away, they are stained bright red.

"That's a demon!" Henry is bellowing. "That's a demon!"

"I kind of got that!" Tresser replies, watching it swoop in a high arc through the corridor. There's nowhere to go except down or up—and down only leads to one place. The creature does not want to end up in the Pits, so he's going to come back. He's going to head *up*.

Up to the fight. Up to Nathan.

From the sound of things on Nathan's end, the battle has descended into chaos. What will happen if this rogue agent ends it once and for all?

That thing was locked up in a cell for a reason, Tresser realizes. It is not like other demons; it is not a demon at all. It is a monster, and it will destroy everything in its path. Alliance or Legion, good or bad. Enemy or Nathan.

Henry has Lucy in his arms, supporting her with all his strength. The other prisoners are slumped against the wall, lifeless and pale, but free. They are no longer bound to their doom. They're safe, for what it's worth.

As long as the monster doesn't come back.

There is no time to think. Tresser only has the chance to act.

"Call Cassie," he demands. When Henry meets him with a startled gape, he repeats it. "Call Cassie, now! Tell her to pull you all out!"

"What the hell, Tresser, no! What about you?"

"I have my own comm," Tresser says, tapping the device in his ear. His attention is not focused on Henry, however; it's trained on the shadow of the flying beast steadily swooping back up the corridor towards them. If he can distract it, they might stand a chance. If he can lead it off course, away from the vulnerable prisoners, away from Nathan and his army...

If Tresser can lead it to the Pits, the monster is done for.

There's no way out. There is no other magic on their side; he knows no spell, no exorcism, no weapon capable of killing that thing. There's only one way to destroy it: to lead it down.

The shadow is close enough that he can almost touch it. He casts a frantic Henry one last determined nod. "Call Cassie and get out of here," he echoes.

Then, without another word, he takes off down the corridor.

CASSANDRA IS ON the ground bleeding, and Malephor's attention is torn between that and the literal *chaos* around her.

The demons themselves aren't the hard part. They're all low-level privates, overconfident and undertrained, determined to seize their chance and raise the human world. She cuts them down before they get the chance. Malephor works lightning-fast, lashing out with claws and teeth, slaughtering the demons in her wake before they get a chance to wreak havoc.

Still, it is not enough. Cassandra is hurt. It is not enough.

Adam is at her side, holding her up and dragging her towards the side of the room. Cassandra has a hand pressed to her face. Her messy hair is matted with red, the same liquid that spills from between her fingers. Blood, Malephor realizes, and her adrenaline surges. She is not worried; she is *furious*. How *dare* they harm Cassandra? How dare they lay a single filthy claw on her?

She will obliterate them all.

Cassandra suddenly claps a hand to her ear, rocketing upright. Malephor's first thought is that she has been hurt again (her rage sends her claws skewering through a shapeshifter's chest), but Cassandra proves her wrong the next second. "It's Henry!" she exclaims over the chaos. "He needs to get out!"

Adam is already scrambling to his feet. "Do they have the prisoners?"

"Yes, yes, all of them—they've got—"

Cassandra suddenly freezes; the blood drains out of her face. She looks like she's been attacked all over again, and Malephor is so startled by the strong reaction that she nearly misses a demon swinging at her head. By the time she takes care of him, and his two friends, Adam and Cassandra have already scrambled over to the spellbook at the far end of the room.

Cassandra is frantically flipping through pages, while Adam half-heartedly tries to stop her. "We have no choice!" he exclaims. "We've got to get everybody else out!"

"We can't do it!" Cassandra fires back. "We can't leave Tresser behind!"

THEY FIGHT LIKE hell, but it's not enough. It *isn't enough.*

Nathan doesn't see his first man fall, but he hears him when he hits the ground. It is with a hollow thud, and then—silence. Silence where there was harsh breathing at his back, emptiness where seconds ago was the presence of life.

Over his shoulder, someone stumbles---Havricc, just a private. Blood is pouring from his mouth like a fountain; he's been cut down by a sword to the chest and a blast of concussive energy aimed straight at him. He was dead as soon as he hit the ground, but there's still so much blood— it's *everywhere.*

One of Nathan's men, dead, right at his back. Gone before he saw it coming.

He can hear more—the sounds of his men shouting for their comrades, the gasps and cries of pain as the battle begins to turn against them. He sees Mestorros fall with a mace caught in his leg. Janec topples, a sword catching him in the head.

He's losing them. He's *losing.* Horror wells in Nathan's throat, and he can't breathe, he can't *think* except to fight. He can feel the adrenaline brimming under his skin, straining to burst out, to destroy everything around him. This was *his* plan. This was his mission.

He cannot be the cause of his unit's destruction.

A Grey gets too close to him, and Nathan doesn't think. He lashes out, catches the Grey by the wrist, and *drains*.

The Grey's settled form erupts into an explosion of dust, drawn into Nathan's own body. There is nothing left of him—no energy, no ashes. *Nothingness.*

Interitus.

"Nate!" He hears Tresser's voice straining to reach him over the comm, but there is no time to focus on him now. *"Are you okay? Nate?"*

Nathan absorbs the energy of three more Greys who are going after Chorso. One second they're rushing towards him, and the next they are gone. Nathan *feels* their energy inside of him, charging him up, spurring him on. He can still feel their final emotions—blind determination and fury.

The Legion is so sure they will not lose...but they already have. They *are* going to lose. It doesn't matter what enemy tries to stand in its way—pure destruction will always win.

Two Greys firing at Appolis's position—gone. Three others lunging for the fallen Mestorros—vanquished. One with his sword swinging towards Abraxas's throat—no more.

Nathan feels each bit of energy as it is pulled inside him. These are lives, he realizes—demons, centuries old, High Demons and low, dying at his hands. This is his power as it was meant to be used: blind destruction.

It should not feel good, but it *does*.

He is desperate. He is determined. His men will not meet their deaths here, on his orders, on a suicide mission. This will not be how Unit X is remembered; they will live to fight another day. They are good enough, brave enough, and Nathan—

He is Naberos, Knight of Hell. Naberos is *Interitus*. He is destruction. He will reap, and kill, so they can live.

A charging mass of Greys is vanquished in the blink of an eye. The pressure bearing down on Nathan's body grows more and more intense. Breathing is a struggle; thinking is almost impossible. He recognizes friend from foe, but he can do little more than that. Their enemies are rapidly dwindling. Unit X starts to outnumber the Grey foes, and Nathan can feel himself ready to explode.

There's so much adrenaline inside him. He has never felt like this. The rage, the fury, the hatred, the ferocity— it all brews into a numbing cocktail, threatening to crush him to dust. He is ready to combust under the weight of it all. This was what he was meant to do, he knows, but so much destruction—

It's so much. It's too much. He can't take it.

He is on fire. He is going to explode.

HIS LUNGS FEEL ready to combust in his chest, and his entire body protests the exertion he's forcing it through. He's never run this hard in his *life*.

Tresser's a borderline alcoholic who lives out of his car, but he spends most of his time chasing after monsters. He might not get the chance to visit the gym often, but he's by no means an unfit guy. He can outrun a raptor, chase down a galloping hellhound, and track a bloom of flying jellyfish through the countryside without breaking a sweat.

But this goddamn *thing* is giving him a run for his money.

He sprints around another sharp turn and hears the shrill bellow of the creature at his heels. Its shadow follows just a few paces behind him, harsh against the light that increases the further down into the tunnels they go. It is no longer a bird; now the creature is an apelike hellion that propels itself from wall to wall almost faster than Tresser can run. Every so often, it swipes at his heels. Tresser feels the thing's claws graze him, endures the prickle of his flesh at the sheer evil which radiates from it, and pushes himself a little faster.

It's following him. This is a good thing. As long as it's following him, it won't get to Nathan.

Only it sounds like Nate has bigger problems upstairs—and try as Tresser might, he can't raise a response from him. He might not be able to be there in person, but he can hear everything. He cannot escape the sound of Nathan's labored breathing in his ears. The hellion's screeches can't drown out the roar of battle over the comms, or the exclamations of vaguely familiar voices as they call out Nathan's name.

Whatever's going on up there, it sure sounds like Nathan has taken control of the battle. That must be a good thing, right?

He can hardly breathe, but he forces himself to speak into the comms again. "You've gotta come through for me, Nate. Let me—let me know what's happening."

There is no reply. This is how Tresser knows that it's bad. If Nathan were okay, he would say something in return; Nathan always, *always* says something.

Something is very wrong.

RETURNING TO EARTH is not like leaving it the first time. When they escape, they are not going through a portal; instead, they are being pulled out all at once, like being sucked up through a vacuum. Henry feels his skin prickle with gooseflesh first; a second later, the surrounding tunnels explode in a brilliant flash of ultraviolet light. He feels his senses detach from his body, and all at once, he is spiraling through nothingness; the only real thing is the solid body he grips in his arms.

When he slips back into himself, he is sprawled on Cassandra's living room floor, and Lucy is still in his arms.

She's so limp. God, she looks lifeless. Her hair, always a luscious mass of golden curls, now hangs matted and filthy over her face. Her cheeks are hollow, eyes sunken and bruised. All color has drained from her, like an old photograph; her skin is white, covered in black bruises, and the blood streaming along her body is so dark it almost looks black as well. There's so, so much blood.

She looks *dead.*

The thought pulls a sob from Henry's throat, and he cannot help cupping her face in his hands. The shallow, reassuring rhythm of breath from her parted lips is the only thing that lets him believe that she is alive.

The feeling of a hand on his shoulder is the only thing that jerks his attention back to the real world. Adam is running back and forth between the various bodies crumpled on the floor around them. There is an older woman, a battered young man, a boy who can't be more than a teenager...they all lie, battered and bloodied, in no better shape than Lucy.

They stole their lives, Henry thinks, desperation and panic welling up in his throat. *They took them away and drained them. They stole everything.*

He grips Lucy tighter in his arms. She doesn't stir. Her body is cold.

Cassandra pulls her hand away from Henry once she sees he's back with them and turns her attention to the other victims. She pauses at the sight of the young man with ginger hair and stubble lining his pallid cheeks; her own face drains of color. "Josh," she mutters, as if the name has come to her in a dream. "His name is Josh."

Adam doesn't glance up at her, too busy taking the pulse of a middle-aged man. "A friend of yours?"

She shakes her head. "Not me," she breathes. "A friend of a friend."

Henry's heart is racing; he can taste it in his throat. He feels seconds away from vomiting and turns away on instinct to avoid getting any on Lucy. Instead of sick, however, words come spilling out his mouth, faster than he can stop them.

"Tresser's still down there. I had to—we had to leave him, we had to, we—we let something out. Something really bad. He led it away...he's going down. Nathan—"

That's all he can bring himself to say. He does not know where Tresser and Nathan are, does not know how they're doing. In this moment, they're unreal to him. The only thing that matters is the broken body in his arms.

He presses his forehead to Lucy's, unable to hold back his sobs any longer. "Please," he gasps. "Please don't leave me."

NATHAN LOOKS DOWN at his hands again and cannot recognize them as his own.

They are no longer cracked and brittle; now they are pulsing. White light is bursting from his nail beds; his knuckles are luminescent. His entire body is vibrating, energy rolling through him like the ocean in a storm. He can feel each wave, each crest, each roar of the untamable tempest. It is all *inside* of him.

Still, he draws in even more. Each enemy that comes at his unit meets their end within seconds. They do not have time to think, to feel, to fear. He lashes out at them and sucks them in.

He feels them vanish beneath the force of his power, like crushing dirt to dust in his hands. Energy is such a pliant thing. He lashes out at an enemy aiming for one of his men's heads, and the Grey freezes. His entire body tenses; veins stand out in his temples, his neck and face flood crimson as if he is about to burst. In the next second, he shatters, leaving only the energy that flows into Nathan's body. After that, nothing, nothing. There is nothing left.

Nathan takes them all, and leaves none to fear.

He destroys and destroys, without mercy, without thought—until finally, there are no more enemies. Only his own men, staring at him in horrified awe.

Nathan takes a shallow breath and hears it echo in his lungs. His heartbeat is thrumming throughout his entire body. He can taste his stomach in his throat. Everything is overloading all at once; he is overheating, broiling inside of himself. His insides feel like they're about to turn into his outsides, his brain is turning to liquid, there *is no air* in his lungs—

Is this what it feels to have all the energy sucked out of you at once? Does it hurt this much? Does it *feel* like you're going to die?

He tries to take a breath but can't. He tries to speak but can't. He's going to burst, and he *can't do anything.*

"Nate!"

The shout comes from his comm, but for a delirious moment he convinces himself that it doesn't. He imagines footsteps pounding against stone floors, a familiar figure turning the corner, stepping up to him without hesitation. He cannot recognize the face his mind summons, but his instincts scream that he is not a threat. He is a human, this strange hallucination. How strange. A human, and a friend.

His voice echoes in his ears again, and somewhere in the back of his screaming mind, Nathan remembers. *Tresser.*

That doesn't make sense. He shouldn't be here. He should have *left* already, done his job and then gotten to safety—

Tresser exhales a breath. When he speaks, he sounds strained, frightened. *"Nate,"* he mutters, and the word drowns inside Nathan's too-full chest. *"What the hell did you do?"*

Minutes ago, Nathan couldn't hear a word being said over the comms; now, Tresser is all he can hear. One of his men says something, but Nathan neither understands nor cares. He can only focus on Tresser. Tresser, with his ragged breaths, and the face that, even when imagined, makes Nathan feel safe. In Nathan's hallucination, Tresser is trembling. He is afraid of monsters, but he fights them; he has never allowed himself to look afraid. Nathan has not seen Tresser show real fear before and doesn't know what it would look like.

In his dream, Tresser is looking at him, and he is afraid.

Nathan yearns to take a breath. His lungs are frozen, unwilling and unable; he does not know how to fight against them. The phantom of Tresser takes a step forward, and Nathan cannot speak up to stop him.

(He can't get too close. He will destroy him. He is a living weapon. All he knows how to do is destroy.)

"What's wrong?" Tresser asks softly. Nathan squeezes his eyes shut; he still sees Tresser against the black of his eyelids.

"The energy," he grinds out. "Too...much...all of it..."

"There's too much inside you." Tresser can always read between the lines. Nathan explained his powers to him; he knows their dangers, knows Nathan's own fears. When he speaks again, his tone is low and reassuring, like a balm to Nathan's raw nerves. "It's okay. We're going to fix this. You've just got to keep breathing, Breathe for me, Nate."

He can't. He *can't.*

A small gasp escapes his throat, more of a whimper. Tresser lets out a gasp of his own; but if he's in pain, he doesn't let on. *"I know you can, Nate. Come on. You're stronger than this. You're stronger, remember?"* The phantom is beseeching, desperate. He takes another step, reaching out for a glowing hand, but Nathan jerks away just in time. *"You can do this."*

Nathan is almost sure that he can't. "Tresser—" He gasps, and then a burst of pain drowns everything else out. For a moment, it overpowers him. When he comes back to himself, he is not sure he's back at all. There is a white-hot pulse in his chest, ready to destroy him.

He doesn't think he can fight it.

NATHAN IS DYING.

Tresser, can feel it; can hear it, as definitely as he can hear the monster racing behind him. The tunnels are growing hotter now, almost unbearable, and Tresser feels as if he's running through fluorescent hallways instead of cavernous tombs. Everything is so much brighter; it all seems amplified around him. The pounding of his feet against the ground; the harsh sound of his own voice as he pleads with Nathan; his racing heart.

It's all so real, and he's not sure why. He is afraid to find out the answer.

The tunnels only go so far. There are no more cells lining the walls. The air feels charged with electricity, static and heavy, like it's ready to smother him. There isn't an ounce of uncertainty in Tresser's mind; he knows exactly where he's running.

Dread pools in his stomach, but he cannot succumb to it. He cannot slow down; he cannot stop. The creature on his heels can't be allowed to reach Nathan.

(Even if the battle is over, this thing is still a demon. If it attacks Nathan, Nathan will kill it: and if he takes on so much energy, he will surely die. Tresser will not, cannot, allow this thing anywhere near Nathan.)

So, he runs. He runs, and runs, and hopes the tunnels will not come to an end.

Even through the burning in his lungs, he forces himself to talk, because he knows he is the only thing Nathan has. He is the only thing he can hold on to, and he needs to ground him. He's got to bring Nathan back to himself before it's too late. He has to remind Nathan of who he is—more than a weapon of mass destruction.

"You talked Henry down when he was panicking, remember? You agreed to help him—when you had your own orders to follow. You stopped Lehexe and me from killing each other. You planned this out because…because you wanted to help. You came to earth because you were the best man to lead this mission. You were the only man who could, Nate. That's all you. Not your powers. That's *who you are.*"

His feet draw to a stop of their own accord. He can't run anywhere. There is nowhere else to run.

Oblivion stretches out before him, pure and senseless.

The Pits are a cavern of white, churning and swirling like a luminescent ocean. There is nothing human about them. They are, at once, both the most natural and unnatural things that have ever existed. A part of Tresser isn't sure they do exist; they simply are, and there is no comparing them. There is no way for him to comprehend them, but he is frightened. An icy fear settles in the pit of his stomach, swells up and overflows to fill his chest, his limbs, his mind. He has never been more frightened in his life.

"Don't let go of that," he whispers. "You gotta hold on, Nate."

A billion stars dance in his vision. The Pit extends hungry arms, reaching up for him. Over his head, a black shadow swoops down, and tumbles into the Pit with not even a screech.

Tresser sees the demon vanish and feels its existence be snuffed out like a candle flame. It is a tangible feeling of existing one minute, then being nothing the next. It is more powerful that Nathan could ever be. The Pits consume as if nothing has ever existed at all.

The Pits are the end. The Pits are all there ever has been.

The Pits are taking him.

"I TRUST YOU," the voice over the comm gasps. Tresser sounds like he's crying. *"I believe in you, Nate."*

He sees Tresser's phantom hand reach out and seize his. Their fingers twine between one another's; Tresser grabs hold and squeezes, grounding Nathan like nothing else could. *I trust you,* he says again, and the words reverberate in his ears. *I trust you, I trust you, I trust you.*

Nathan takes a deep breath and remembers what air tastes like. He opens his eyes.

There is no Tresser in front of him. The gossamer strands of his dream are whisked away like a spiderweb. He is left staring down at his battered company. Unit X is worse for wear after the battle, but they still gape at him; they stare as if they are watching their leader implode in front of them. None of the men dare breathe. No one moves a muscle.

"The energy," Nathan murmurs, feeling the steady burn inside of him. It no longer hurts; he is no longer panicked; but there is still all there, every bit, and it is destroying him from the inside. "There's too much. I can't handle it."

"You've got to get rid of it somehow." Tresser's voice echoes, as if through a tunnel. *"What can you do?"*

"I don't *know.*" Nathan needs to do something, fast; it's destroying him.

"Okay. Okay..." Tresser breaks off, silent. When he speaks again, he really does sound like he's crying. *"You've gotta use it, Nate."*

"How?"

There are no good answers. Tresser knows this; even Nathan, in his overwhelmed, agonized haze, can recognize it. Nathan doesn't know what he can do with so much raw power, or even if he *can.* Tresser knows this;

Tresser always understands what he's thinking without him having to say it. Tresser understands the helplessness, the frustration, the terror that Nathan is feeling. When he speaks again, it shows in his trembling voice.

"Use it, Nate. You've got to make it count. Use it for good." A shuddering breath, and then an exhale. *"I believe in you."*

Nathan clings to these words as if they are all that exists; as if he is falling into the Pits, and they are the last thing he has to hold on to, his only lifeline. Nathan closes his eyes and is sure of exactly what he must do. There is no great realization. He has known it all along.

Nathan lets go.

FAR AWAY, ON the boundary between reality and what never existed at all, Tresser does too.

SOMEWHERE BEYOND THE barrier between the human and demonic realms, many people open their eyes at once.

Grey eyes open to a cold, stone room that feels like the crypt it is, a white dress, and blooming flowers clutched between clasped hands.

Eyes as human as the earth itself open to rope burns around wrists, a burning in strained lungs, and the memory of two friends cowering in the ruins of a bar.

Brown eyes behind broken glasses open to the dust-filled ceiling of a darkened apartment, smudged chalk stains on the ground, and the echo of a last kiss upon chapped lips.

A hazy set of blue eyes, clear as a summer sky, open to the caress of a lover's hand, a warm lap, and a shuddering breath that feels like fire.

"Beck?" The exclamation is a whisper. It barely dares to hope. "You're—you're alive."

Beck Murray forces himself to sit up, unaware that many others do the same in the exact same second. For the second time, he shakes the last clinging echoes of death from his groggy mind.

"Yeah," he says after a moment of consideration. When he smiles at Adam, it is like the dawn breaking over a pitch-black night. "I think I am."

Epilogue

IT'S GOOD TO be able to breathe again.

When he steps outside, his lungs are immediately flooded by a rush of fresh air. It carries the sweet, rich tang of the countryside, mixed with something more familiar. This is what Cassandra calls an *"autumn breeze"*. Having never experienced earth's seasons before, he has no idea why the taste of September air reminds him of a home he never had.

This, Nathan supposes, is just another of the human world's many wonderful quirks.

It's just on the cusp between summer and fall, and earth is changing around him. The leaves are shifting to a vast canvas of crimsons and golds, illuminating the world in a lasting sunset. Afternoons grow cooler by the day. Soon, Cassandra says, it will be too cold to leave the house without a jacket.

Nathan has never experienced cold weather before, so he'll just have to trust her. He's not sure how well he's going to handle winter on earth, but so far, his first autumn is beautiful.

"There he is," Henry crows, catching up with him and throwing an arm around his shoulder. "The runaway bride! We thought you decided not to come join us. I was about to send Mal in there to sniff you out."

Nathan looks into the grinning face of his friend and fights back a smile of his own. "She's not a guard dog,

Henry," he replies. Of course, it's a little hard to tell at times with the way Malephor can be found in Cassandra's shadow more often than not. That doesn't give Henry license to employ Malephor for all the other things he's been trying to put her to use for—from getting things down off of high shelves to intimidating some of his more obnoxious colleagues at work.

("I'm friends with a demon now," Henry said. "Why don't I make the best of it?")

To her credit, Malephor has done what Henry's asked every time. Nathan considers it might be possible that spending so much time on earth has made Malephor more sympathetic to humans than she lets on.

"Come on," Henry tells him, guiding him towards the rest of the party. "Lucy just chased all of us guys away from the grill. You are not gonna believe how good she can make a burger. It's like heaven in a bun, your mind is going to be blown!"

Nathan shakes his head, huffing in amusement, as he lets himself be swallowed up by the crowd. It's not a massive group—Nathan isn't sure how many people the backyard of Cassandra's house could hold—but he's able to recognize each face anyway. Cassandra has never been the social type, but since they've returned to earth, she has somehow gained a whole host of new friends, from a variety of places.

It started out with Nathan moving in; just to help with repairs around Cassandra's house. Opening up a portal to hell in the middle of her living room and then closing it again had done a number on Cassandra's place. Slowly, his presence there became normal, even comfortable. The human world seemed a much more welcoming place, after all that happened down below.

Nathan assumed that he could find peace here. Just Cassandra and himself, living in quiet.

This didn't last, of course. When you're friends with Henry Lee, *quiet* is a hard thing to find. Cassandra, Nathan, and Malephor started joining Lucy and Henry for nights out; they also became better acquainted with Adam Lehexe, and his rowdy band of New Jersey college students by extension. Meeting George Soto was perhaps the most surprising thing, considering his surprising connections both to Cassandra and Unit X's own Sergeant Valac.

Not that there is a Unit X anymore. The war is over; there was no need for elite fighting units. Every one of his men who survived the assault on Gehenna got to go home, and Nathan is proud of it.

They didn't end the world singlehandedly, of course; but the destruction of the Fortress of Gehenna did a number on the Righteous Legion. Not long after Gehenna fell, so too did the entire Quadrant Seven. After that, the enemy fell around them like dominoes; only the Demoniac Alliance, and all it stood for, was left standing.

Not to mention the human world; which, had the Legion won, would not have been the case.

It was a very good thing, then, that they were able to destroy Gehenna at all. The mission was so dangerous, so costly, that at times Nathan wonders if it was worth it. Then he remembers the moment he learned the war was at its end. He sees autumn leaves changing colors around him, listens to his friends laugh around the dinner table, hears a strain of a song he remembers playing over the hearse radio...and he knows it was.

Everything that happened down in Gehenna had to happen. He hates it. The knowledge claws at his insides every day, constricting his heart, stopping just short of strangling him. Still, Nathan knows it was worth it.

If they hadn't fought, there would be no more human world. There would be no more Labor Day weekends, and no more barbecues in Cassandra's sprawling, sunlit backyard.

Nathan's eyes survey the scene before him, and he smiles to himself. After a long summer of recovering, this all could not feel more natural. On one side of the yard, an animated Beck Murray is chattering with Cassandra, while Malephor pours lemonade a few feet behind them. Towards the other side, Nathan catches sight of Lucy, her blonde curls pulled behind her head into a ponytail, sharing a joke with Adam Lehexe in front of the barbecue.

He doesn't make any effort to join the crowd. Instead, he seeks out the old oak tree on the far end of the yard and finds a place beneath its shade. This is a comfortable place. He always comes here when he is looking for answers, or to make sense of his thoughts. Cassandra tells him the tree is ancient; its energy is older than the house, than the rest of the woods surrounding them. When she speaks of the tree, there's a certain reverence in her eyes.

Nathan can't feel any of that. To him, it's just a tree; but sometimes standing under it makes him feel a little closer to human.

The music is loud, and the chatter is louder, but beneath the oak, Nathan feels like he's found his own pocket of peace. He smiles, allowing the comfortable atmosphere to wash over him. It's not every day they can all get together like this.

Alyssa, in a bright purple sundress and oversized sunglasses, is not just alive; she *pulses* with it. A shy smile is on her lips as she sways to the music with her friend

Sophie, and a few of George Soto's friends. Sophie has her head tossed back, laughter bubbling through the air. Josh, one of the men Henry pulled out of hell, twirls her.

The scene is practically idyllic. Everyone is here. Everyone is present, happy, *alive*. Everyone except...

The gate opens with a click of a latch, and Nathan's head snaps in that direction. *There* he is. Late, just as expected.

GEORGE DEFINITELY ISN'T late—he's just fashionably on time.

("You're gonna miss the whole party," Jack was sniping at him not half an hour before. "It started already. Come on."

"All right, all right, I'm coming." George rolled his eyes but didn't turn away from the air conditioner in front of him. He had today to fix it; its owner plans on stopping by tomorrow afternoon. Getting a handyman business off the ground is hard, but not impossible as long as he gets the work done on time.

He fixed the machine perfectly. Now he just needed to lay on the finishing touch. George laid his hands on both sides of the air conditioner and felt the pulse of power through his wrists. His eyes flashed black—just for a second. It happened quickly, but it was long enough. A tiny jolt of demonic energy courses into the machine, and George felt it come to life beneath his palms.

Tomorrow, the air conditioner will start perfectly. It will never leak again, never sputter and die...and if it cools the entire house, what's wrong with that?

George grinned to himself. His job isn't the only thing that's new; but superpowers are only great if he puts them to good use.

"George," Jack said, laying a hand on his shoulder, and George knew it was time to go.)

He stomps into the party like he owns the place and is greeted by a round of cheers. Even Cassandra grins in greeting—poor Cassie, who's going to have to clean up this mess once everyone's done. He'll stick around for a while after the party to help, George decides. He owes it to her. He sure made a mess of this house while he was staying here.

"George Soto!" James Petrucello claps him on the back, jarring his entire body. "You really dragged your ugly ass all the way out here?"

"If you didn't get to look at my ass, you'd miss me," George replies. James's grin stretches across his entire face. When he swings out an arm, he briskly catches Dana around the waist, but she's been by his side the whole time anyway.

"I've got my favorite ass right here. I don't need to look at anyone else's."

"Good answer," Dana smirks, and reaches out to steal George away. "Hey, honey. You look great. How've you been?"

"Ah, pretty great. Never felt better, actually."

"I'm glad." Dana's red-lipped smile is nothing but genuine. Jack grunts next to George as James greets him in a similar way; Dana and George exchange rolled eyes at their respective partners' over-the-top social habits.

The couples hit it off as soon as they met, but it's not such a surprise that Jack's first human friend would be a guy like James Petrucello. He's not afraid of anything; that's something Jack can respect.

George can't help but grin as he watches Jack settle into a comfortable banter with his friend. It makes him happy that Jack is growing more comfortable around humans. Double dates and coerced social interaction have been doing their job well—not to mention, it gets George out of the house more.

"I didn't think you were topside nowadays," Dana remarks, quirking a fine-pointed eyebrow. George smirks at her.

"Just got back. We couldn't miss the party!"

As much as George has been trying to get Jack accustomed to Earth, they only spend half of their time here. It didn't take long after George woke up for them to realize that things weren't...*exactly* as they left it.

A soul isn't something you can get back, once it's gone. Without it, George supposes his body needed a bit more fuel to start itself up again. The demonic energy that brought him back did its job well, but unlike with the others, it never really left him. The fact that George wound up resurrecting as more of a demon than human doesn't bother him one bit.

He'll admit, Hell's a wild place. They sure know how to party down there. It's a whole new world to explore, interesting people to meet, dangerous adventures to go on...in a way, Hell is exactly what George was looking for. As long as another civil war doesn't start up any time soon, he thinks he could be comfortable in Jack's world. That doesn't mean he doesn't want Jack to be comfortable in his own.

("I love you," Jack told him the first time George's eyes turned black. "I'll help you deal with this however you need me to."

"Just...be here for me," is all George said. "We'll figure it out together.")

There are worse things than having superpowers—having superpowers *alone*, for example.

Not that George is ever really alone.

"Finally decided to show up, huh?"

He's nearly bowled over by the force of another body slamming into his, but he wouldn't be able to fall anyway. Matt is on one side, Josh is on the other, and they're both grinning like it's their birthday party instead of a Labor Day weekend bash. "Took you long enough," Josh chimes, ruffling George's hair. When a disgruntled George pulls away, they both laugh.

"They're on a sugar high," Alex pipes up from where he's nursing a beer near the snack table. He raises his drink to George in greeting before holding another can out to him. "Great to see you, buddy."

"Figures that as soon as he falls in love he forgets all about us," Matt chimes, plucking Alex's beer out of his hands and taking a sip before passing it back to him. "What happened to camaraderie? Brotherhood?"

"*Brothers* don't get frisky with each other in the back of movie theatres."

"Legally," Josh adds, then shudders. "Last time I ever third-wheel with you two, Soto."

George grins, unashamed. It had been Jack's first trip to the movies, and they made it a memorable one. He feels Jack come up behind him and is just aware of his presence before strong arms loop around his neck.

"Hey, guys," Jack says to George's friends, who all raise their drinks to him in turn.

It was weird at first, adjusting to everything. Josh still has nightmares about his time in hell; Matt remembers very little from being possessed, and Alex still has panic attacks any time he remembers the bar explosion. But once they all got over the novelty of no longer being dead and/or tortured, they were all happy to get back to normal; even if their new normal now included George's demon boyfriend.

Dana might know, because she figures out everything; but George still hasn't told them that he came back different. They don't need to know. For now, at least, he wants everything with his friends to be as normal as possible.

Life after death is proving to be pretty good for George. He's got old friends, new friends, superpowers, and a guy he can't believe loves him back. What more could he want?

"So," Jack says, leaning close to George's ear. "Don't they usually have cake at parties?"

"HOW'S IT GOING with the cake?" Cassandra calls over her shoulder. Malephor looks up at her, a smear of frosting on her chin, and gives her a thumbs up.

She tries to hide her grin, but she's sure she doesn't succeed. Malephor's brows furrow as she looks at her. "What is it?"

"You've got—no, not quite—ahh, oh my gosh. Okay, here." Cassandra moves in quickly, licking her finger and brushing the frosting off of Malephor's dark skin. She doesn't realize how quite like her mother that just was until she pulls back to find Malephor staring at her with wide eyes.

She no longer has George Soto's ghost whispering in her ear, but she hears the real thing over her shoulder. "Way to go, Cassie!" George crows, and Cassandra feels her face heat up.

"There. It's gone," she says belatedly, offering Malephor a crooked smile. The demon nods hastily and goes back to cutting the cake.

Things are never awkward with Malephor. Cassandra certainly wouldn't call them easy—they're still feeling each other out, trying to decide what exactly they think of the other—but she knows enough about the demon to be sure of two things. She likes Malephor very much, and she would trust her with almost anything.

Today, she is trusting Malephor with the cake. The night before, she trusted her with secrets, uncertainties and fears that Cassandra has never felt close enough to anyone to share before. In her profession, friends are hard to come by. People like Mal, who look at her and *see* her, are even rarer.

Malephor does not see the scar gouged deep into her cheek—the one reminder of the portal opening that Cassandra will never be free from. She runs her fingers along its serrated edges, but looks straight into Cassandra's eyes. Cassandra's chest is tight, her lungs frozen, her heart still.

They do not understand each other completely, but they're getting there, little by little. Mal visits the human world frequently, now that there is no longer a war to win. Cassandra always has snacks ready, and something to drink. They're cycling Mal through various juices now to find out which one's her favorite. So far, she likes cranberry.

She still seems determined to protect her. Cassandra doesn't know why. She has proven to Mal that she is not weak, and Mal has proven to her that she cares for more than military orders. Yet their friendship has sustained, in spite of the worlds that separate them. If Cassandra is being honest, she wouldn't be happy with anything less. Things are tentative and a little uncertain, but if Cassandra knows one thing for sure it's that Mal is worth getting to know.

"Hey!" Henry suddenly swoops in, already reaching for a slice of cake. Mal is too quick—she slaps him away before he can manage to pilfer one. Henry draws back with a pout, which quickly morphs into amusement again when he catches Mal's smirk.

"You can wait like everyone else," Cassandra sing-songs, and Henry turns his grin on her.

"IT'S NOT FOR me! It's for Lucy!"

He hadn't really expected he'd get away with a piece—not with the way Malephor was guarding the cake like a hawk—but Henry figured he'd try anyway. Lucy asked for cake, so Henry was going to do his damnedest to get some for her.

He flutters his eyelashes at Mal, to no avail. The demon has a heart of stone. When he turns to Cassandra, he's hoping for a better reaction, but she just shakes her head.

"Patience, dear Henry. We haven't even eaten dinner yet."

Lucy's busy with that. Henry's gaze strays over to the grill, where his wife *(wife!* it's still impossible to believe) is laboring, sweat glistening upon her brow and burger grease staining her bright blue top. There is a look of determined focus on her face; she wields the burger flipper like a professional. Her hair is pulled into a knot at the back of her head, and her lips are pursed into a thin line.

She's beautiful. Then again, Henry always thinks Lucy's beautiful.

His mind flashes back, unbidden, to the Pits of Gehenna. The sight of Lucy hanging off of a stone wall, her wrists and feet bound in heavy iron chains, had sent a shock wave of terror through his body. The blood that dyed her golden curls a sick crimson; how her skin was coated in sweat and grime; the way she hung forward, motionless. Most awful, however, was the way she didn't even stir when Henry cried out her name.

She'd been through hell. In that second Henry couldn't think of how beautiful Lucy was. He couldn't remember how much he loved her. He couldn't even realize how relieved he was to have finally found her.

The only thought in his mind was that if he lost Lucy now, he didn't know how he could go on living.

If he lost Lucy then, he would rather have died, instead of...

He shakes himself out of his haze, and feels his grin grow a bit brighter, defying the memories. "Dinner's coming up," he tells his friends. "Just be ready with the cake afterwards!"

Cassandra rolls her eyes, and Henry sends them a wink before making his way across the yard. Lucy glances up before he's even halfway there. He catches a flash of pearly teeth, a distracted wave, before she's focused on her grilling once more.

"Need some help?" Henry asks as he reaches her side. She casts him a grateful look.

"Please. Plates, and napkins—the condiments are all set up, right?"

"Everything is there for you, don't worry," Henry chuckles as he grabs a handful of plates. He knows the idea of a hot dog without mustard will make Lucy riot. Henry is a ketchup man to his core, and they've had that argument more times than he can count. Three times since Lucy got back, and he's relished every traded barb.

Lucy murmurs a thanks and directs him as to how to set up the table. He lays out plates, rolls, chips, and anything else they could need. When Lucy looks over, she flashes a satisfied grin and swipes the back of her hand across her forehead.

"Nice teamwork," she murmurs, "husband."

"Couldn't have done it alone, wife," Henry replies. The word sends a thrill down his spine, and he knows Lucy feels the same way.

They're married. In a lot of ways, it's impossible to believe, but it's true.

The date they had set for their big white wedding was the day Henry pulled her out of Hell. Circumstances changed, brides went missing, so obviously things couldn't go as planned, but the last thing either of them wanted to do was forego their marriage.

They had a small, quiet ceremony at city hall a week later. There was no time to summon the wedding party. Lucy got one of her coworkers to be her witness, while Henry asked Cassandra. That night, they went home man and wife.

There was no great party, no orchestra, no crowd of joyful families. There was just Henry in a suit, Lucy in a simple white dress, and their signatures on a piece of paper. It was everything they needed.

Things aren't always easy. Lucy was weak for a long time after her imprisonment, making up for what the demons took from her. They stole more than her freedom; they took her blood, her energy, her confidence in her ability to protect herself. When she wakes up in the middle of the night screaming, Henry soothes her. They've signed up for self-defense classes together. Lucy is teaching him how to defend himself against demonic attacks and has promised her exorcist days are behind her. Things aren't easy, but they are good.

Henry couldn't be happier, and he's sure Lucy couldn't be either. He'd say they earned their happily ever after, but the truth is they're nowhere near the ending yet. They've barely begun.

A loud crash jars Henry's attention and causes him to nearly drop the plate in his hands. He glances over his shoulder to find—to his utter unsurprise—Beck Murray sprawled on the ground, limbs flailing like an octopus.

"JESUS CHRIST," JAMES hisses, grabbing Beck by the arm and hauling him back to his feet. "You tryin' to get yourself killed again?"

Beck grumbles as he twists out of James's grip. It's not as if he was *trying* to land on his ass. He was sure he could do that cartwheel—and he probably could, before his third beer. He's not drunk, not even close, but his balance is off, and he feels lighter than before.

It's a good feeling. The buzz leaves him warm and happy with the world at large. He can't even bring himself to scowl at James for long. Dana tosses a potato chip at his head and Beck grins as his best friend's face twists in disbelief.

"Leave 'em alone," Dana laughs. "Not like much can keep him down at this point anyway. He's gonna keep coming back no matter what we do."

Beck beams proudly in the face of James's exasperated eye roll. "Great. Figures we'd end up with the Beck the Immortal Fuckin' Ginger."

"That's *Amazing* Immortal Fuckin' Ginger," Beck retorts. James snorts.

"Watch it. One more brainless stunt and *I'll* put you in your grave, 'n make sure you stay there."

"Good luck with that," Dana snorts over the edge of her beer can. She fires another chip at James's face; her aim is off, and gets it caught in Beck's hair instead. As he scrambles to free the crumbs from his hair, his friends' cackling follows him. He doesn't manage to dodge the noogie James aims his way.

It's good to be where he belongs. It's good to be home.

He finally contacted his family a few weeks ago. He didn't bother calling; instead he made the long drive to New Jersey himself, with James in the passenger's seat, Dylan and Adam sitting in the back. It was the most chaotic road trip of Beck's life. He's pretty sure Adam hexed Dylan into silence more than once. James has the most obnoxious music tastes of anyone he's ever met; and as soon as the sun goes down, he can't drive without becoming a hazard to himself and others.

Even so, they somehow made it there without anyone killing one another.

Beck showed up on his parents' doorstep and nearly gave his mother another heart attack. She was frailer than he remembered, older, with more gray in her hair and defined lines on her face; but her hug was still tight as ever.

Explaining everything was long and difficult. He's glad he wasn't alone. He's especially glad that Adam was there.

And now, things are mostly back to normal. Beck has started college again. His mother calls him at least once a day, and he's still working at Adam's shop. His second (or third?) chance at life couldn't be going better.

He's got his family; he's got his friends, and he's got Adam.

His eyes seek out Adam in the crowd. They do that whenever they go places, and somehow, he always finds him with ease. Even now, it's as if his gaze is drawn to him. He spots familiar dark skin and darker hair without even having to search. Before he realizes what he's doing, he's already moving to Adam's side.

Adam is looking on, a small smile on his lips, as Sophie and Alyssa manage to corner Dylan. A part of Beck is surprised that both girls grew so fond of Dylan; then again, it's not surprising at all. Dylan was one of the first people able to coax Alyssa out of her shell. Now no one's better at getting her to break into laughter, not even Sophie—except at her most determined. Dylan's friendship with Alyssa was what first caught the attention of a newly revived Sophie. It wasn't long before Dylan became one of *her* favorite people. She loves to fuss over him, like he's a particularly cute puppy and she's his owner. Dylan acts like it bothers him, but Beck knows the truth: he's eating up the attention from two pretty girls.

Beck isn't jealous. He's got Adam to give him all the attention he needs.

He rolls his eyes as Dylan appears very interested in whatever Alyssa is showing him on her phone. When he mutters something, Alyssa breaks into a wide grin. Seeing her so unguarded—*carefree*—is becoming more and more common these days. Every time she creeps a bit further out of her shell, Beck feels a rush of pride for his friend.

Alyssa's recovery is a lot more complicated than his own, but she's strong, and she's putting herself together piece by piece.

Of course, she's got Sophie to help. Sophie takes care of Alyssa in any way she can. She takes care of Beck, too—hell, Sophie takes care of Adam. She's good at taking care of *everyone,* and ever since she and Adam became business partners, she's had more opportunities to get closer to Beck and his group.

Working at a bookstore/witchcraft supply shop is an experience like no other. Sophie handles the more magical aspects of the business, while Adam is still most comfortable surrounded by his notes and bookshelves. Beck helps wherever he's needed. Working there has gotten even more exciting now that he gets to meet a variety of magic practitioners. Plus, he gets to spend all the time he wants with Adam. That's definitely the greatest benefit to his continued employment at the bookshop—even if he devotes a lot of time and energy to keeping Adam from working himself to death.

"You look tired," he mutters, nudging Adam in the shoulder. "Were you up late last night?"

Adam scoffs. "Beck, I'm up late every night."

"Not tonight." He twines an arm around Adam's shoulders and, heedless to anyone who might be watching, presses a kiss to his temple. "I'll stay over. You can come to bed early with me. We can fall asleep watching movies, just relaxing…it'll be nice."

"Movies?" inquires Adam.

"Rom-coms. As many as you like. You can choose."

Adam hums with pleasure, the sound vibrating against Beck's chest. "That sounds fantastic."

"Let's do it, then." Beck grins into the crown of Adam's hair and relishes the chuckle that rumbles in his boyfriend's chest. "You and me."

"If I didn't know better, I'd think you had something else in mind."

"Well...we can see how the night goes, right?"

Stress relief is important. Adam works day and night at his job, constantly pushing himself to study and learn more. Beck is a busy college student too, and nighttime excursions with *RAVES* only add more to his plate. (Now that there are fewer demons on earth, there's not much for the exorcist squad to do—but if there's one thing they're good at, it's finding trouble.) Moonlighting as an exorcist is fun, but Beck is grateful to have a normal life to return to in the daytime.

"It'll be nice," he coaxes, wrapping his arms around Adam's shoulders and pulling him closer. Adam leans in without protest, supporting his weight against Beck's chest.

It's a quiet sort of intimacy, but that's what they're best at. This is the peace Beck has found with Adam, and he wouldn't trade it for the world.

He loves Adam. He loves his friends. He loves his life and everything about it.

It's great to be alive.

IT'S NATHAN'S FIRST human party, and he enjoys it.

The burgers are as good as promised; the cake is even better. He savors each bite, never able to get enough of human food. When he's finished his plate, Cassandra rolls her eyes and gives him her leftovers.

"You'll need it for the road," she mutters. Nathan, not missing the sad undercurrent to her words, gives her shoulder a squeeze.

Once the food has been eaten, the beer and soda goes the same way. People mill around, dancing and talking, enjoying one another's company in the way that only humans can.

This entire party is so quintessentially human. Nathan closes his eyes and allows the atmosphere to wash over him.

Tresser would have enjoyed this.

He wouldn't have admitted it, of course. No, god forbid anyone ever knew David Tresser was having fun. He would have sat beneath the ancient tree with Nathan, sipping a beer and watching his friends with poorly masked fondness. "You know," he probably would have said, "we have too many friends." Nathan would have rolled his eyes, chuckled, and relished the feeling of the breeze on their faces.

If he closes his eyes, he can almost hear the whisper of Tresser's voice; almost feel the phantom brush of a hand against his; but the dream of Tresser vanished at the same moment as Tresser himself.

Instead, Nathan sits under the tree alone.

Instead, Tresser led a monster into the Pits of Hell...to protect Nathan. Tresser lost all of himself to the Pits. Nathan was able to save everyone else. He could not save the person he wanted to most.

While Nathan was using the massive amount of energy to destroy Gehenna and revive the humans lost in the great conflict, David Tresser was pulled into oblivion.

He's been through guilt. He's been through blame. In the first few weeks, his grief was so intense that he almost let it destroy him. He could hardly face Unit X. He could not stand to return to Hell, return to the world and the regime that was his life. He holed up in Cassandra's home and tried to lose himself in the foreignness of the human world.

It was Cassandra who finally pulled him away from the edge of his own Pit. She sat him down and grieved with him; she reassured him; she insisted, again and again, that it was not his fault. Nathan did his best. Nathan saved so many people.

Nathan did all he could.

But he did not do *enough.*

Tresser deserved more than living out of his car, working under his father's thumb, chasing monsters he wished he didn't have to believe in. Tresser, so smart, so perceptive, so determined. Tresser, who cared more than he would ever let on. Tresser, who understood Nathan more in two days than any demon had in a hundred millennia.

Tresser lulled Nathan into falling in love with him so easily that he didn't realize it was happening until it had.

Tresser deserved to be happy.

If there were any way for Nathan to save him, he would. If there were any fragment of Tresser left, even a whisper, a cell, a mote of dust...he would pursue it to the ends of all the worlds. Cassandra, however, searched days and nights for any trace of him, and was finally forced to confirm what Nathan already knew.

The Pits give nothing back.

"You have to find peace," Cassandra told him at last. "That's the only way you can heal."

There is no recovering from David Tresser. Nathan can never forget him.

All he can do is live.

Slowly, the party's flame dwindles to a smolder. George's friends are the first to leave; they're followed by Adam and Beck, the college kids, Sophie and Alyssa. George Soto lingers to help clean up the party, but it's not long before he's ready to go as well; with a nod to his old commander, Valac escorts his human away.

Lucy vanishes inside the house. After a murmur from Cassandra, Malephor follows; her eyes linger on Nathan until the door closes behind him. Finally, the yard is empty except for Cassandra, Henry, and Nathan.

They stare at each other for a moment before Harry breaks the silence. "Are you ready?"

Nathan hauls himself to his feet, stepping out of the oak tree's shadow. "Yeah," he says. "I am."

The darkening sky has cast a veil of shadow over Cassandra's long driveway. Nathan follows in her footsteps, hearing twigs and gravel crunch beneath his feet. Steps in Hell left an audible trail; it was always like walking on nothing. This is a unique distinction of Earth, and he loves it.

The human world is different from anything Nathan's home ever was. Here, he is something different; but not a person to be feared. In the human world, he does not bear the weight of his gifts. He is not a pariah. He is not *Interitus*.

For the first time in his life, he does not have to constantly work to prove himself. Nathan is shocked by how free he feels.

They stop at the top of the driveway, next to a long black car. The hearse is practically an institution, at this point. Its driver stepped out of it and never returned. It has rested in the same spot for months.

Not for long.

"So. Nate." Henry scuffs his shoes in the gravel. "This is going to be the last time we see you for a while, huh?"

Nathan smiles, and shakes his head. "I'll be back. I'm not leaving forever."

"You sure aren't." Cassandra reaches out, looping her arms around Nathan's shoulders, and squeezes him tight. The warmth of her hugs is as familiar to him now as the bitterness of coffee in the morning, or the crickets chorusing in the night. It reminds Nathan of a new home—one he never imagined he'd find.

"Don't be a stranger," she whispers. "You need anything, you call me. I'll probably know anyway...but call. You hear me?"

"I will." Nathan returns her hug, as tight as he can without hurting her. "Thank you, Cassie."

She draws in a breath at the familiar nickname. "Find peace," she mutters.

Peace. The only thing he can hope for.

Nathan heaves a sigh that causes his shoulders to rise and fall like the swell of a wave. This is necessary for the both of them, but that won't make leaving his new life behind any easier. It doesn't mean he's eager to drive out into the world alone; it doesn't make him ready to find the head of Tresser Corporations and deliver to him both his son's car and his tragedy.

Tresser's father deserves to know, though, because in a way he must have loved his son. This is the only way Nathan can find peace. It's the only way he can let Tresser go.

There is no forgetting him. There is no leaving him behind. There is only the hope of a peaceful future in a new world.

It's what they all need.

Henry reaches up, clapping Nathan on the shoulder. When Nathan looks down at him, he's reassured by the resolute expression on his friend's face. Should he need anything, he has Henry's number and his confidence. He will never be alone. Somehow, he has become a part of this absurd family, a mixture of human and demonkind. No matter how far he goes, he'll always have a place to return to.

Nathan will do it for Tresser. He'll do it for Cassandra, for Malephor, for Beck and Adam, for George, for Harry. He'll do it for himself.

He slips into the front seat of the hearse and nods at his friends. Henry and Cassandra step to the edge of the driveway, waving him away.

Nathan rides off, chasing the last flicker of sun on the horizon. The car is solid beneath him. In the seat next to him, he imagines another body, as tangible as a whisper; the ghost of Tresser vanishes as easily as he was never there at all.

Any world is filled with darkness. Human or demon, alive or dead; there is something black and unknowable within all of them. It is inescapable. It lurks in the darkest corners, inside of closed caskets, concealing nightmares and secrets. Darkness will always exist, and it will always destroy.

It is also capable of creating *incredible* things. Not all darkness is dangerous; sometimes, the darkness can provide safety. Sometimes, it can protect. Sometimes, it gives back.

Often, the most beautiful things can be found outside of the light.

About the Author

Emilie Lucadamo has too many stories, and not enough words to tell them. At eighteen years old, she has been writing for most of her life, and telling stories even longer. Her dream is to one day become a critically acclaimed author. When not writing, she's probably reading, or spending quality time with her dog.

Twitter: @EmilieLucadamo

Website: www.emiliesbooks.tumblr.com

Other books by this author

In the Darkness Series

How We Sell Our Souls

The Cost of Living